Cousin Trouble

Linda glanced around the Lockwood Fairgrounds and asked, "Where's Carly?"

Kathy nodded toward a tree. Her nine-year-old cousin was stretched out in the shade. "At least she isn't wrecking anything," Kathy said. "Maybe the whole day will go easy."

But what if something did go wrong? Linda knew that being in charge of six ponies was a lot of responsibility.

Just then, Linda felt a strange nibble behind her. She whirled. Nacho, the Shetland pony, was nuzzling her back pocket, searching for a carrot.

"Nacho! What—" She looked up. Lollipop was ambling toward the carnival games, and Bandit was grazing by the side of the drive.

Linda grabbed Kathy's arm. "The ponies!" she cried. "They're loose!"

Books in The Linda Craig Adventures series:

Available from MINSTREL Books

THE LINDA CRAIG ADVENTURES #12

KATHY IN CHARGE

By Ann Sheldon

A MINSTREL® BOOK

PUBLISHED BY POCKET BOOKS

New York   London   Toronto   Sydney   Tokyo   Singapore

A MINSTREL PAPERBACK *ORIGINAL*

A Minstrel Book published by
POCKET BOOKS, a division of Simon & Schuster Inc.
1230 Avenue of the Americas, New York, NY 10020

Copyright © 1990 by Simon & Schuster Inc.
Cover art copyright © 1990 by Susan Tang
Produced by Mega-Books of New York, Inc.

ISBN: 0-671-67476-5

First Minstrel Books printing March 1990

10 9 8 7 6 5 4 3 2 1

THE LINDA CRAIG ADVENTURES is a trademark
of Simon & Schuster Inc.

LINDA CRAIG, A MINSTREL BOOK and colophon are
registered trademarks of Simon & Schuster Inc.

Printed in the U.S.A.

KATHY IN CHARGE

1 ◆◆◆

"Let's do something *really* neat for the Lockwood Elementary Fair," twelve-year-old Linda Craig said to her best friend, Kathy Hamilton. They were sitting next to each other in the noisy school cafeteria. Linda was unwrapping the sandwich she'd packed for lunch.

"Sounds good to me," Kathy mumbled, her mouth full of pizza. The freckle-faced blond swallowed with a gulp. "Do you have any ideas?"

Red-haired Marni Brown set her tray on the round table and slid into a chair across from her two best friends. "You ought to hear what Amy's doing!" Amy was Marni's younger sister. "She and her friends are setting up a dunking booth at the fair. And guess who's getting dunked?"

"My brother Bob?" Linda asked hopefully. She

1

brushed her long black hair behind her shoulders and opened her carton of milk.

"No, even better." Marni's eyes twinkled. "The teachers."

"The teachers!" Kathy and Linda squealed together.

"Yeah. If you hit the target with a baseball, they drop into a vat of cold water."

Linda leaned forward. "Do you think Ms. Gifford will volunteer?" she asked.

"Let's hope so!" Marni said. Ms. Gifford was their sixth-grade teacher and their riding club instructor, and boy, was she tough!

"You know, a dunking booth's a great idea," Kathy said wistfully. She tugged at a strand of her blond hair. "I wish we'd thought of it."

"Oh, come on," Linda said. "We can think of something even better."

"There's always a bake table." Kathy's face brightened. "We could sell our famous chocolate chip cookies. You know—like we did with the Cookie Express." At one time the girls had raised money for their friend Kelly Michaels by baking cookies and delivering them on horseback.

Linda and Marni looked at each other and groaned.

"No hard feelings, Kathy, but I've baked enough cookies to last a lifetime," Linda told her friend.

"Besides," Marni added, "standing behind a table and watching people pig out on cookies all day isn't my idea of fun."

"Well, then, why don't we do something with our horses?" Kathy suggested. "You could teach us some new stunts, Linda."

Marni burst out giggling. "Only if you think people would pay to see me fall off," she said.

"Get real, Kathy," Linda added. "We have only eight days to get ready. Those tricks I learned for the last fair took me weeks and weeks."

"Well, at least I made some suggestions." Kathy slumped into her chair and picked at her cold pizza. "That's more than you guys have done."

"Hey, we were just teasing." Linda shot Kathy a concerned look. "Are you all right? You seem kind of down."

With a sigh, Kathy tore off a small piece of pizza and slowly munched it. "Yeah, I guess I am feeling down. My aunt Betty and uncle Paul are coming to visit for a couple of days."

"You didn't tell me that when you invited me to spend the night," Linda said.

"They're not coming until late." Kathy sighed again.

"Don't you like your aunt and uncle?" Marni asked, puzzled by Kathy's reaction.

"Aunt Betty and Uncle Paul are great. It's their bratty kid, my cousin Carly, that I hate." Kathy angrily bit off another hunk of pizza.

"She can't be that bad," Marni said, watching Kathy attack her food.

"Oh, yeah? Remember last summer? I was grounded for a week because I wasn't keeping the barn clean. It was Carly's fault. She deliberately messed it up after I spent hours raking and sweeping.

"And remember when all the sugar and salt in the restaurant got mixed up? Well, guess who got blamed, and guess whose fault it really was."

Kathy sat up, her face flushed. "And then there was the time she dumped cereal all over the kitchen floor and put a snake in my parents' bathtub and—"

Linda raised her hand. "Okay, we get the picture. She's a brat."

"How old is this terror?" Marni asked.

"Nine. Which means she's too old to boss around but too young to take care of herself. I just *know* my parents are going to ask me to watch her." Kathy groaned. "My weekend will be ruined."

"Maybe not." Linda patted her friend on the shoulder. "Marni and I could help."

"Leave me out of this," Marni protested. "One younger sister is enough for me."

"Maybe we can volunteer Carly for the dunking booth," Linda suggested jokingly.

"No, she won't be here long enough to ruin the fair." Kathy smiled at the thought.

"Which reminds me, what *are* we going to do to raise money at the fair?" Linda asked.

"I like Kathy's idea about doing something with our horses," Marni said.

"But what?" Linda asked.

Marni shrugged. For a few moments the three thought in silence.

"What's Jackie doing?" Kathy finally asked. Jackie Lee was one of their best friends.

"She's back in class finishing an English assignment for Sarge." Sarge was the girls' nickname for Ms. Gifford.

"No, I mean what's she doing for the fair?"

"Oh, she and the Hombres are going to play Saturday night."

The Hombres were a band made up of Linda's fifteen-year-old brother Bob, Bob's best friend Larry Spencer, and Jackie.

Kathy giggled. "They'll make a lot of money for the Special Kids Fund. People will pay big bucks *not* to hear them play."

"Hey! That gives me an idea." Marni sat up just as the bell rang for recess. "The class of special kids sometimes goes to Glen Manlon's ranch to ride the ponies. Ms. Gifford's their instructor—remember she was telling us about her special training? Why couldn't we do that? Give pony rides, I mean. Only we'd give rides to everyone."

"Neat idea!" Linda gathered up her trash and tossed it into the can. "All kids love to ride."

"All except Carly," Kathy said. She picked up her tray and headed across the cafeteria. "She thinks horses are big and smelly."

"Boy, Carly sounds like a real pain," Marni said to Linda. "I wish we could help Kathy somehow."

"Me, too. But right now let's work on our idea. We need to ask Ms. Gifford if we can do it."

Instead of heading for the playground, the three girls dashed down the crowded hall to their classroom. Jackie was just handing her paper to Ms. Gifford, who was a tall, pretty woman with blond hair.

"Next time, Jackie, come to class prepared, and you'll finish sooner," Ms. Gifford said sternly.

"Yes, ma'am." Jackie turned and rushed past the girls, a look of relief on her face. "See you outside," she whispered.

Kathy pushed Linda forward. Linda stumbled over the carpet to Ms. Gifford's desk.

"Yes? What can I do for you, Linda?" The teacher's face softened. Ms. Gifford had taken Linda under her wing and taught her and her horse how to jump. Ever since, she'd had a soft spot for Linda and her talented palomino, Amber.

"We . . ." Linda paused. Turning, she beckoned to Kathy and Marni to step forward. "We have a great idea for the fair." She told the teacher their plan about selling pony rides. Ms. Gifford nodded in approval.

"I'll be happy to help, provided you talk to Mr. Manlon, everyone's parents approve, *and* your grandfather takes responsibility for bringing the ponies to and from the fair."

"Bronco will be glad to," Linda said. Her grandfather, Tom "Bronco" Mallory, had already offered to help the girls any way he could. Linda and Bob had lived on Rancho del Sol with their grandparents, Doña and Bronco Mallory, ever since their parents died several years before. The ranch was in southern

California and had been in Doña's family for generations.

"We can ask Mr. Manlon's permission this afternoon," Kathy chimed in.

"Good. When everything's settled, let me know." Ms. Gifford ushered them from the classroom. "Now hurry outside—recess is almost over."

"Pony rides will be so much fun!" Kathy exclaimed as she and Linda walked down Lockwood's Main Street. The two friends were headed to the Highway House, the restaurant and gift shop owned by Kathy's parents.

Since Kathy had invited her to spend the night, Linda had ridden Amber to the Highway House that morning. She'd stabled Amber next to Kathy's pinto horse, Patches, then walked with her best friend to school. That way the two girls could ride in the afternoon.

"I'll ask Bronco if we can use Nacho," Linda said. Nacho was Rancho del Sol's Shetland pony. "He's getting so fat and lazy. A little work will do him good."

Kathy laughed. "Poor Nacho! He won't speak to you for a week!"

Linda laughed with her friend. She was glad to see that Kathy was over her lunchtime blues.

Suddenly Kathy stopped dead in her tracks, and her smile turned into a frown. "Oh, no," she groaned loudly.

"What's wrong?" Linda looked where Kathy was pointing. A blue van was parked in front of the Highway House. It had Arizona license plates. "My aunt and uncle and Carly are here already."

She gave Linda an anguished look. "Let's tell my folks we have to ride right over to Flying Star Ranch and ask Mr. Manlon about the ponies. At least then I won't have to face Carly until dinner."

"Sure. If you think it'll help," Linda replied.

Feet dragging, Kathy headed up the walk. Linda followed behind. It was midafternoon, and the restaurant wasn't yet open for dinner.

Linda could hear laughter coming from inside. Kathy shot her friend a warning look. Then she plastered a smile on her face and strode into the main dining room of the restaurant.

Kathy's parents were seated around a large circular table. Across from them were Kathy's aunt and uncle. They called hello and hugged their niece. While they were exclaiming at how much Kathy had grown,

9

Linda looked hard at Carly, the terrible troublemaker. She was sitting quietly next to Mrs. Hamilton. With her angel face, long brown hair, and a sprinkling of freckles across her nose, she looked completely harmless. Not at all like the brat Kathy had described.

"Look what your aunt and uncle brought you," Mrs. Hamilton said to Kathy. She held up a T-shirt covered with turquoise, purple, and blue swirls.

"Wow! Thanks." Kathy gave them an extra hug.

"And I have one just like it!" Carly piped up. "We'll look like twins."

"Won't that be cute?" Mrs. Hamilton introduced everyone to Linda. "How about a piece of cake?" she offered.

"I'd love one." Linda took an empty seat next to Carly. When she passed Kathy, her friend nudged her and gave her a look that said "watch out."

Linda began eating her cake. As always, Mrs. Hamilton's desserts were out of this world. While she chewed she glanced over at Carly. The nine-year-old flashed her a shy smile. Linda couldn't help but smile back. With her upturned nose and pink cheeks Carly looked like a little china doll.

Linda heard a funny rasping sound. Kathy was clearing her throat, trying to catch Linda's attention.

"Careful!" Kathy mouthed. She gestured toward Carly.

"She's cute," Linda mouthed back. Kathy pretended to gag.

"Kathy? Kathy!" Mr. Hamilton called his daughter's name. "Are you all right?"

"What? Me? Oh, yeah!" Kathy flushed bright red.

"As I was saying, your aunt Betty and uncle Paul are going on a cruise to the Bahamas. They'll be leaving tomorrow, so they won't get to stay the weekend."

"That's great!" Kathy exclaimed. "I mean," she added quickly, "that's great about the cruise. It sounds really neat."

Mr. Hamilton continued with a big smile. "But the best part is that you and Carly will have so much time together. Carly is staying here for those two weeks!"

2 ◆◆◆◆

Kathy's mouth dropped open. "Carly will be here for *two weeks?*"

"That's right," Mrs. Hamilton said. "Won't that be fun?"

"Two weeks?" Kathy repeated in a stunned voice.

Mr. and Mrs. Hamilton nodded, and Kathy's aunt and uncle beamed as if they'd just given her wonderful news.

Linda stole a glance at Carly. The nine-year-old was sipping her soda. Could Carly really be that bad? she wondered. Or was Kathy making a big deal out of nothing?

"You'll have to look out for her after school and some evenings while your father and I work," Mrs. Hamilton added. "Not that Carly needs much watching. She's grown into such a young lady." She stroked her niece's long hair. Carly flashed her a bright smile.

"But—but—I can't!" Kathy sputtered, looking back and forth at her parents. "I won't! The fair is coming up, and I made all these plans. I won't let Carly mess things up—like she always does!"

"Kathy!" Mr. Hamilton said in a shocked voice. "You apologize to Carly—and to your aunt and uncle."

"That's right, young lady," her mother said sternly. "That was rude and uncalled for."

Kathy stood up so fast her chair almost fell over. Her face was flushed, and her lower lip quivered. "I'm sorry, Aunt Betty and Uncle Paul, and—and—" She paused and her eyes narrowed as she looked at Carly.

Linda turned. For a second she thought she saw a nasty grin on Carly's face. Then it disappeared, and Carly again looked as sweet as an angel.

"I'm sorry, Carly," Kathy finished in a low voice. She spun on her heel and dashed from the dining room.

"Excuse me." Linda stood up. "It was nice meeting you all. Thanks for the cake, Mrs. Hamilton." Then she hurried outside. She knew right where Kathy was headed.

Linda clattered down the porch steps and ran around the big building. The Hamiltons had a small barn and paddock in back, where Kathy kept her horse, Patches.

A nicker greeted Linda as she entered the barn. Her mare, Amber, stuck her head over the stall door and shook it as if to say, "About time you got here!"

Linda gave Amber a quick kiss on her velvety nose. Then she peered into Patches's stall. Kathy had grabbed a currycomb and was furiously grooming the pinto's brown-and-white coat.

"He'll go bald if you don't slow down," Linda teased.

Kathy turned to face Linda. "Now do you see what I mean? Carly's been here twenty minutes, and I'm already in big trouble." She sighed and began combing Patches's mane. "I can't believe it. Two weeks. It'll be terrible."

"Oh, come on, Kathy. It can't be that bad." Linda picked up a brush and went into Amber's stall. The golden palomino nuzzled her arm, then reached her long neck down for a bite of hay. "Carly's kind of cute."

"Cute!" Kathy snorted. "You *can't* agree with my parents. That's all I need."

"Well, maybe she's old enough now to hang around and not be such a pain."

"She'll always be a pain. You wait and see. She never wants to do anything, she hates horses, and she's always whining. And what am I supposed to do with her while we're getting ready for the fair?"

"Maybe she can make signs for us or—"

The screech of a rusty door hinge made Linda stop in midsentence. Kathy peered over at her with a finger to her lips.

Kathy tiptoed across the stall, and Linda followed her down the aisle. Right before the open door of the barn, Kathy stopped. She waited for Linda to catch up with her. Then the two of them sprang outside.

Carly was hiding behind the barn door. She jumped up in surprise when she saw the two girls. Then she took off running for the Highway House.

Kathy ran after her and caught Carly by the back of her blouse. She yanked the younger girl to a halt.

"What do you want, you little sneak?"

"I'm no sneak! Wait till I tell my mother what you said." Carly slapped at Kathy's hand.

"Go ahead. I'll tell her how you were spying on us. And I have a witness." Kathy pointed to Linda, who was standing by the barn.

15

Carly glanced at Linda, then looked back at Kathy. "You better not tell my mom anything or—or"—she smiled nastily—"or else."

"Or else what?" Kathy retorted, but Carly jerked from her grasp and ran the rest of the way to the house.

The two friends watched in silence as Carly leapt up the back steps. Before she went inside she turned and stuck her tongue out at Kathy.

Kathy gave Linda an I-told-you-so look.

Linda shook her head. "I'm sorry I didn't believe you. She *is* a little brat."

Slowly she and Kathy walked back into the barn.

"Two weeks," Kathy muttered to herself. Then she brightened. "Come on, let's ride out to Flying Star Ranch. I need to forget about Carly."

The two girls went back into the barn. Linda slid her western saddle off the rack. Her bridle was hanging from the saddle horn, and her blanket was wrapped over the top of the saddle.

Linda opened Amber's stall door. Amber pricked her ears and eagerly stamped her hoof. Linda threw the striped blanket onto the mare's back and smoothed it. Then she carefully set the heavy saddle on top.

Amber turned her head to stare at her with big

brown eyes. "Always ready to go, huh?" Linda teased. Amber nodded, and her creamy white forelock flopped up and down on her white star.

Linda knew exactly how her horse felt. All day Amber had been cooped up in a stall. And all day Linda had been cooped up at school. They were both ready for some action.

Linda tightened the girth, then slipped the bridle from the saddle horn. She looped the reins around Amber's neck and put the bit in the mare's mouth. Next she slid the headstall over Amber's ears and smoothed the mare's silky forelock. She buckled the throatlatch, and they were ready to go.

When she led Amber from the barn, Kathy was already mounted and waiting outside.

"Boy, you're an eager beaver," Linda said.

"Sure. I want to get away from Miss Sneaky." Kathy reined Patches toward the wide path and kicked him into a fast trot.

"Hey! Wait up!" Linda stuck her left foot into the stirrup, swung her right leg over Amber's back, and settled into the saddle. Amber twirled and leapt into a canter. Gathering up the reins, Linda slowed Amber to a trot.

"Whoa!" she cried. "You don't have to be an eager beaver, too!"

Amber settled into a comfortable jog, and the two girls rode happily side by side. Ten minutes later they cantered up the dusty road to the Flying Star Ranch. After a recent fire had damaged one of the stables, Glen Manlon, who owned the ranch, had had the barns and sheds brightly painted. Fat ponies grazed contentedly in the pasture.

In a small corral just ahead they saw their friend Kelly Michaels. Kelly was exercising her beautiful coal black mare. As usual, she was riding bareback. Linda waved, and Kelly reined her horse, Cinder, over to the fence. Linda and Kathy hurried their horses to meet her. Amber reached the fence first. She touched noses with Cinder and nickered a horse hello.

"What're you guys doing here?" Kelly asked. Kelly worked at the ranch after school.

"We need to talk to Mr. Manlon. We want to borrow some ponies for the fair," Linda replied.

Just then a broad-shouldered man wearing a cowboy hat strode toward them.

"Hello!" Glen Manlon greeted them. "What brings you girls to the Flying Star?"

Linda launched into her story. When she was finished, Mr. Manlon tilted his hat back and smiled. "That's a super idea. The school's special class only rides here once a week." He nodded toward the grazing ponies. "Those lazy critters could use some extra work." He winked at Linda.

Kelly's eyes sparkled in excitement. "Ms. Gifford said some of the money we raise will be used so the kids can ride twice a week," she said. "So the ponies will get their exercise!"

"Why don't you girls come over tomorrow and help out," Mr. Manlon suggested. "You can meet the ponies then."

"Good idea," Linda and Kathy chorused. They said goodbye, then turned their horses toward home.

Back at Kathy's they quickly untacked the horses and rubbed them down. They turned Amber and Patches into a grassy corral to graze. Patches put his head down and hungrily attacked the grass, but not Amber. She sniffed and snorted until she found the dustiest spot in the corral.

Folding her legs under her, she lay down on her side. Then, kicking her hooves in the air, she rolled back and forth until every inch of her glossy coat was covered with powdery dirt.

"Ugh," Linda groaned. Amber scrambled to her feet and shook the dirt off. She seemed to give Linda a hurt look.

Kathy laughed at Amber's antics. "Come on," she said to Linda. "Let's see if dinner's ready. I'm starved."

The girls ran up the steps and through the back door of Highway House. As the screen door slammed behind them Mrs. Hamilton called out Kathy's name. Kathy gave Linda a worried look. Her mother's tone of voice hinted she was in big trouble.

Kathy and Linda burst into the big kitchen where meals for the restaurant were prepared. "We had to ride to Manlon's—I'm sorry I forgot to tell you, but I can explain everything," Kathy said, the words tumbling out.

Kathy's mother frowned. Carly was sitting in a corner, sniffling. Aunt Betty was trying to comfort her.

Mrs. Hamilton held up a small multicolored T-shirt. In the middle of the shirt was a big purple stain.

Kathy looked at the shirt, then at her mother. "What happened?" she asked.

"That's what we'd like to know, young lady."

"You think *I* spilled juice on Carly's shirt?"

"No. Carly explained what happened. When we saw the rip in her blouse, we realized why she spilled the juice. She was upset because of the fight you two had."

Aunt Betty pushed Carly gently from her chair, then turned her around so her back was to Kathy. A two-inch tear split Carly's frilly blouse.

"How could you do that?" Mrs. Hamilton asked. "I think you'd better explain."

Shock and embarrassment reddened Kathy's face. Linda tried to remember what had happened when Kathy grabbed Carly. Had the blouse really ripped? She'd been too far away to see.

Linda caught a glimpse of Carly peeking from behind Aunt Betty's skirt. Carly was smiling smugly at Kathy. So that's what she'd meant by "or else."

"But I didn't rip her blouse!" Kathy exclaimed.

"Carly didn't rip her own blouse," Mrs. Hamilton said gently. "Why don't you go up to your room and think about it?"

"But I—I—" Kathy stammered. Then she saw Carly's expression. For a second their eyes locked.

"All right, don't believe me," Kathy said through clenched teeth. "As long as Carly's here, I don't care if I stay in my room for the whole two weeks!" Turning on her heel, she ran from the kitchen.

3 ♦♦♦♦

Linda stared after Kathy in dismay. She wasn't sure what to do. The blouse might have ripped when Kathy grabbed it. She couldn't honestly tell if Carly was pulling a fast one.

"I'd better take you home, Linda," Mrs. Hamilton said, interrupting Linda's thoughts. "I'm sorry you can't sleep over."

"That's okay. It won't be dark for a while. I can just ride Amber."

"Well, then, I'll call Doña and tell her you're on your way."

She walked Linda to the back door. Carly was happily eating a double-scoop ice cream cone. Aunt Betty was hovering around her.

"I'm sorry about this," Mrs. Hamilton said quietly.

"I don't know what happens to Kathy when Carly visits. I was hoping this time they'd try to be friends."

She opened the back door for Linda. "Maybe you can help. Try being nice to Carly and including her in some of your plans." She looked at Linda with a worried frown. "Otherwise it's going to be a long two weeks."

You can say that again, Linda thought. She said goodbye and headed down the steps.

Saturday morning Linda woke to a beautiful, crisp southern California spring day. With a yawn she glanced at the clock. Nine o'clock already!

She scrambled out of bed and slipped into a T-shirt and jeans. Kathy and Marni were coming any minute to discuss plans for the fair.

At least she *hoped* Kathy was coming. She hadn't called. Carly had already ruined their plans for Linda to sleep over at the Hamiltons' the night before. She hoped Carly wouldn't wreck that day's plans, too.

The smell of corn bread drifted into Linda's room. Quickly she ran a brush through her long hair. Then she tied it back with a twisted scarf. She pulled on her moccasins and padded downstairs.

Luisa Alvarez, Rancho del Sol's cook and housekeeper, was clearing the dining room table. Bronco, Doña, and Linda's brother Bob had eaten earlier. "I think I hear two *banditas* in the kitchen," Luisa said to Linda with a wink.

Linda opened the kitchen door and caught Marni and Kathy helping themselves to two warm pieces of corn bread. "Hey! Leave some for me," she cried. She looked around the spacious room and peered out the back door. "No Carly?"

With her mouth full of corn bread Kathy nodded happily. Linda grabbed a glass of milk and a hunk of corn bread and followed her friends outside.

"She's with my folks—sightseeing," Kathy explained. "Carly threw a fit when her folks left. They thought she needed something fun to do. I didn't have to go, though. They agreed our meeting was important."

The girls sat down on the grass in the shade of an orange tree. Linda leaned against the trunk and took a bite out of her corn bread.

"Kathy told me what happened yesterday," Marni said. "I get annoyed with Amy sometimes, but she's an angel compared to Carly."

"Listen, guys, I don't want to hear Carly's name mentioned *all* day," Kathy said. "Let's just talk about the fair."

"Okay. Bronco said he'd trailer the ponies to the fairgrounds," Linda reported.

"Then everything's covered," Marni said excitedly. "We've got the ponies, transportation, and Ms. Gifford to sponsor us."

"Not everything," Kathy reminded her. "There's signs and decorations and—"

"—and helping out at Flying Star Ranch this afternoon," Linda finished.

"I can't wait. Kelly loves working there." Marni finished her corn bread and drained the last of the milk.

"Hey, look—here comes Larry." Kathy pointed as a tall boy, fifteen years old, strode up the walk. He was carrying an electric guitar.

"It's too early for the Hombres to rehearse. You'll wake up the whole town," Linda teased.

Larry grinned back as he opened the kitchen door. "At least we're doing something helpful for the fair."

"What's that? *Not* playing?" Linda giggled.

"No," Larry said sarcastically, "*not* selling chocolate chip cookies."

"For your information, we're not selling cookies this year," Kathy told him. "We're giving pony rides."

Larry guffawed. "Hope your backs don't get sore."

He slammed the door and disappeared into the house.

"What a comedian," Kathy grumbled.

Linda jumped to her feet. "That gives me an idea. We need a catchy name for the pony rides. Something that will get everyone's attention."

"Great idea—but what?" Marni frowned.

"Let's think while we start making the signs. Mac got us wooden boards and paint, and I have markers and poster paper."

Linda took her glass into the kitchen and gathered up the art supplies. She rejoined her friends, and they hurried eagerly down the drive. Mac, Rancho del Sol's foreman, had laid out brushes, stakes, boards, and bright paints in the shady barn.

Marni opened a can of cardinal red paint. "How about Rollicking Rides?" she suggested.

"Cute. But little kids won't get rollicking," Kathy said. She set a piece of poster board on a couple of straw bales and began sketching horses on the bottom.

"Peewee Ponies?" Linda called over her shoulder. She measured a stake to nail onto the back of a board. They could hammer the stakes into the ground to display the posters.

"Peewee? No way!" Marni and Kathy said together.

They tried out more ideas, but none was absolutely right. They grew silent. Soon the whoosh of paintbrushes and the screech of markers were the only sounds to be heard.

Linda stepped back to view their handiwork. "Wow. Everything looks great—except there's nothing in the middle of the signs."

"Yeah. We'd better think of a name—fast," Kathy said. Hands on their hips, they all studied the posters. They barely noticed when Doña walked into the barn carrying a big pitcher of lemonade and three glasses.

"The signs look wonderful," she exclaimed. Then her expression changed. Doña looked puzzled. "Is something supposed to be in the blank spaces?"

The three girls laughed. Then Linda told her grandmother their problem.

"I see. How about the Pony Place?" Doña suggested. She began to pour a round of drinks.

"Not bad," Marni said. The other two girls agreed. It wasn't as catchy a name as Linda had hoped for, but it had a nice sound to it.

"By the way"—Doña looked at Kathy—"your

mom called. I didn't know your cousin was visiting."

Kathy frowned. "What did Mom want?"

"She wanted to pick you up for lunch. I suggested she drop Carly off here instead. You can all have lunch together."

"Together?" Kathy croaked.

"Carly can help you and have some fun, too."

Linda, Kathy, and Marni exchanged looks that said, "Oh, great."

"Is something wrong?" Doña seemed confused by their reaction.

"No," Linda said quickly. "It was nice of you to invite her." Maybe, Linda thought, Carly would be on her best behavior at the ranch. "But after lunch we have to ride to Manlon's and help out with the special kids."

"Carly might go with you—she's old enough, and I hear they like volunteers." Doña glanced at her watch. "They should be here any minute. Why don't you finish up and come on in?"

When Doña had gone, Marni asked Kathy, "Why didn't you tell her what a pest Carly is?"

"Grownups never believe me." Kathy sighed. "Carly always acts like a goody-two-shoes around them. Then I end up looking bad."

"Doña's right about one thing. We should finish up

these signs." Linda picked up a paintbrush. "Is the Pony Place all right with you guys?"

"Yeah," Marni and Kathy said, but the enthusiasm had gone out of their voices. They printed the name and cleaned up the paintbrushes. By the time they'd finished, the lunch bell was ringing from the backyard.

"That means you-know-who is here," Kathy said gloomily as they walked down the drive to the ranch house.

"Don't worry. Luisa's burritos will cheer you up," Linda said.

The burritos *were* delicious. But for Kathy, lunch was a disaster. Carly was sweet and charming. She had everyone—even Larry and Bob—laughing at her jokes and stories.

Linda glanced over at Kathy. She was staring down at her plate, scowling. Linda couldn't blame her. Carly was making sure everyone thought she was a complete angel.

Linda was beginning to think so, too, when Kathy suddenly stood up. "Let's get the horses saddled," she said to Linda and Marni. "We have to be at Manlon's by one o'clock."

Doña set down her spoon. "Why don't you saddle up Leading Lady for Carly? She's gentle as a lamb. Then Carly can ride with you."

29

For a second Kathy looked surprised. Linda realized she didn't want Carly to come along. Then Kathy smiled. "That's not a good idea, Doña," she said. "Carly's scared to death of horses. She'd better not come. She'd have a terrible time."

Kathy turned and gave Carly a smug look. Then she thanked Doña for lunch and carried her plate into the kitchen.

Linda dabbed her mouth with her napkin, asked to be excused, and followed Kathy to the kitchen. By the time she got there Kathy was already out the door. A minute later Marni sprinted up beside them.

"Hold on, you guys! I didn't finish dessert," Marni said, panting.

"You'll live," Kathy told her. She strode into the barn and swung her saddle off an empty stall door. She and Marni had stabled their horses in the barn that morning. Linda hurried to Amber's stall. She brushed the straw off Amber, then smoothed the saddle blanket on the mare's glossy back.

"Are you trying to get away from Carly?" Marni asked from Midnight's stall. Midnight was a black Morgan.

"How'd you guess?" Kathy called.

"Just a wild hunch," Marni said. "Though I don't know what the big deal is. I thought she was sweet."

A loud groan answered her. Kathy led Patches into the aisle and looked over Midnight's door.

"Don't ever say 'sweet' and 'Carly' together again," she told Marni. She clucked to Patches and leapt into the saddle. As they clip-clopped down the aisle she yelled over her shoulder, "Last one to the stream is a rotten rider!"

With a whoop of excitement Linda tightened her saddle girth. Flipping the reins over Amber's neck, she led her at a trot from the barn. But at the end of the aisle she stopped short. Carly was standing in the middle of the drive. Her hands were on her hips. She was staring at Kathy.

"You better not leave me here!" Carly said, stamping her foot.

"Fine. Okay. Come on," Kathy said sweetly. She reached her hand down. "Grab hold and I'll swing you up. You can ride behind me."

Carly's face grew red with anger. "You know I hate horses!" she sputtered.

"Then stay here." Kathy shrugged. "Maybe Bob and Larry will let you listen to them play."

Without a backward glance Kathy reined Patches toward the cottonwood trail. In a moment they were gone.

4 ◆◆◆◆

"Kathy must be flying!" Marni yelled as she and Midnight cantered behind Amber. "We'll never find her."

"Patches likes to stop at the stream," Linda hollered back. "We'll catch up to her there."

With the wind flying through her hair Linda was enjoying her favorite trail. It twisted and turned, finally taking a sharp left toward a wide, gurgling stream.

She slowed Amber to a walk. Sure enough, Patches was in the middle of the stream, drinking. Kathy was slumped in the saddle, her hands resting on the saddle horn.

Linda led Amber down the steep bank. Amber ducked her head and began sloshing the water with her nose.

"Are you okay?" Linda asked Kathy. "Why'd you take off like that?"

"I don't know." Kathy sighed. "Carly just brings out the worst in me."

"She sure does."

"Whoa!" Marni and Midnight leapt down the bank, landing in the stream with a splash. Midnight pawed the water, then plunked his head in for a drink.

"If this was a race, we just lost," Marni gasped. She gathered up her reins and pulled, but Midnight kept drinking.

"Quit it! I don't want you to get sick," she scolded.

"Patches has had enough, too," Kathy said, clucking to the pinto.

"Wait a minute." Linda reached over and put her hand on Kathy's arm. "Not so fast this time. I think we need to talk."

"About what?"

"About you and Carly. I don't want this whole week ruined just because you and your cousin can't get along."

For a second Kathy pursed her lips together in an angry frown. "Gee, thanks for sticking by me, you guys." Her eyes flashed at Linda and Marni. "How about if I just don't help with the Pony Place? Then your week *won't* be ruined."

"Don't be so touchy. That's not what Linda meant," Marni put in. "It's just that we've been excited about the fair all month. And . . . well, it would be pretty awful if everything was messed up."

Linda nodded at Marni's explanation. "You know we'll do anything to help cool things with Carly and your parents."

Kathy sighed. "I know. You guys are the greatest. And it is *my* problem. I guess I'll just have to work it out."

"With our help," Linda added.

"Does that mean you guys will baby-sit dear Carly whenever I ask?" Kathy gave them a mischievous grin.

Linda and Marni exchanged anguished looks. Then they both nodded reluctantly.

"All right!" Kathy laughed and turned Patches toward the path leading up the bank. "Now let's *ride.*"

The three horses scrambled up the slippery slope. With a whoop the girls raced down the trail.

Ten minutes later they were trotting up the drive of Flying Star Ranch. They were just in time to see a small group of kids and adults getting off an orange school bus.

A girl in a wheelchair was being lowered from the

bus's back door. Since the special class was held at Lockwood Elementary, Kathy, Marni, and Linda knew all the kids by name.

"Hi, Lisa!" Linda called as she dismounted. She led Amber up to the wheelchair. Lisa, a pretty blond girl about nine years old, reached up hesitantly toward Amber.

"Don't worry, she loves attention," Linda said. Amber stretched her head closer so Lisa could touch her nose. "Amber, meet Lisa." Linda pretended to make a formal introduction. "Lisa, meet Amber."

Lisa giggled as Amber blew softly on her cheek. "She's so big," Lisa said in a shy voice.

"A big pussycat is more like it. Look." Linda reached up and scratched hard under Amber's mane. The palomino stuck her head in the air and began wiggling it back and forth.

Lisa burst out laughing. Several people clapped. Amber pricked her ears at the sound. Without a cue or word from Linda, Amber dropped on one knee and ducked her head in a bow.

"Uh-oh." Kathy chuckled. "You'll never get the show-off to quit now."

At the sound of the audience's laughter Amber shook her mane and gave a loud whinny.

"Okay! Enough of the circus tricks," Ms. Gifford hollered. "Let's get to work."

Linda jumped at the sound of Ms. Gifford's barking voice and stared at the teacher. As usual she wore trim, English-style riding clothes that looked out of place on a dusty ranch.

Linda, Kathy, and Marni led their horses into Glen Manlon's barn. After putting them in stalls, they quickly took the bridles off, then joined the others outside.

Kelly had already tacked up six ponies, and several volunteers were on hand to lead the ponies and help each child. A physical therapist was also there to help the kids stretch and relax their muscles.

After brief instructions Linda, Kathy, and Marni were ready to work. Linda was asked to lead Sunshine, an adorable palomino that looked like a miniature Amber. Lisa was mounted in the saddle. Her hands clutched the pony's reins while her legs hung loosely at Sunshine's sides. Her face radiated pure joy.

An experienced volunteer walked beside Lisa. She kept her hand on Lisa's leg as Linda led the pony around the corral.

Ms. Gifford called out instructions from the center

of the small corral. "Riders, put the reins in your left hands. Now stretch your right hands high. Reach back and touch your pony's rump. Now give him a pat. Good!"

After about ten minutes, Ms. Gifford yelled, "Trot!" Linda couldn't believe her ears. But the volunteer nodded for Linda to lead Sunshine faster. The pony took off slowly and steadily. Lisa bounced up and down in the saddle, squealing with delight.

Finally they halted. Linda was exhausted. She felt as if they'd jogged three miles. But it was worth it. Lisa and the other kids had loved every minute.

On the way home Marni, Linda, and Kathy talked excitedly about the fun they'd had.

"After the fair's over, I'm going to volunteer again," Linda said.

"Me, too. The kids are great. Even Sarge was nicer than when she's barking orders at school," Kathy said.

"The ponies were adorable!" Marni cooed. "They'll be great for pony rides. The Pony Place will be a super success!"

Just then Linda felt a drop of water splash on the end of her nose. She looked up. Dark clouds were gathering in the sky.

"Oh, no! We left the signs outside. They'll all be ruined!"

She squeezed her legs against Amber's sides. The palomino danced sideways and then leapt into a canter. Behind her Linda could hear the thumpity-thud of Midnight's and Patches's hooves on the dry ground.

Linda put her weight in the stirrups. She leaned forward as Amber galloped down the trail. Raindrops splattered across her cheeks. Her hair whipped back and forth behind her, and the wind whistled through the cottonwoods. She threw back her head and laughed with joy. Now, *this* was riding!

The three girls burst through the grove of trees and into the yard at Rancho del Sol. They trotted past the riding ring and over to the side of the barn. Anxiously, Linda looked for their signs. They were gone.

"Maybe Mac moved them," Linda hollered. She quickly dismounted and led Amber into the barn. The girls wiped rain from their faces with their sleeves.

They led the horses into the stalls. "Maybe the signs are in here," Linda said. They all looked around, but they couldn't find them anywhere.

"I bet Doña took them into the house." Linda began to untack Amber.

38

"Maybe. But I think I smell a rat." Kathy frowned as she hung her bridle on a peg. "A rat named Carly."

"Oh, come on, Kathy. Quit being so suspicious," Marni called from the tack room. She was wiping off her saddle.

"You don't know Carly! When we left she was as mad as a hornet." Kathy slammed Patches's stall door and started down the aisle. "Anyway, we'll soon find out."

"Kathy, wait!" Linda dropped her bridle and saddle on the barn floor and ran after her. By now she knew that look on Kathy's face. It meant trouble with Carly.

The sound of music was coming from the house. Linda caught Kathy halfway down the drive and tugged on her friend's arm.

"Please—take it easy," she said.

"I will."

But Kathy didn't slow down. She marched into the kitchen. The music was louder there. Someone was playing a guitar while people sang along.

Kathy stormed into the family room. Jackie Lee was strumming her guitar while Larry and Bob were laughing and trying to sing. In the middle of the room Carly was acting out silly motions to the song.

"Hi!" Jackie called. She stopped playing, and everyone looked at Kathy and Linda.

"Gee, real bathing beauties," Larry teased. Linda wiped strands of wet hair off her forehead. She'd forgotten they'd been soaked in the storm.

"Has anyone seen our signs?" Kathy's voice was angry. She glared at Carly. "Because if anything happened to them, Carly, we're going to be real mad."

"Hey! Lighten up." Bob stood up. "For your information, Carly was the one who warned us it was raining. We stuck them in Linda's room."

Kathy's face flushed pink. "Uh—oh, gee," she stammered.

"Hey, thanks, Carly," Linda said cheerfully, hoping to take the heat off Kathy.

"If I were Carly, I wouldn't have been so nice," Larry put in. "You guys just rode off and left her."

"Carly hates to ride," Kathy tried to explain.

"That makes it worse," Jackie said softly. She put her arm around Carly's shoulders. The younger girl leaned against her and smiled sweetly. "You could've shown her what to do. You know, like you helped me when I was afraid to ride."

"We, uh . . ." Now it was Linda's turn to stammer.

She flushed and glanced at Kathy. Even her freckles were bright red with embarrassment. Carly had made them both look bad—and this time it was worse, as Kathy had something of a crush on Bob.

Without a word Kathy spun around and left the room. Linda glanced down at Carly, furious at her for humiliating her best friend. But Carly was smiling so innocently, Linda didn't know what to think.

Linda caught up with Kathy as she headed toward the stairs. Tears glistened in her friend's eyes.

"I can't stand it!" Kathy said, quickly wiping the tears away. "How does she do that to me?"

Linda squeezed her friend's hand. "Well, you did kind of jump to conclusions. Maybe bringing in the signs was Carly's way of trying to make a truce. She could have been really mad when we rode off and left her."

"I guess so." Kathy sniffed. "Maybe you're right. She's just such a spoiled brat. Aunt Betty grants her every wish. And everyone thinks she's so cute, it drives me crazy."

"Well, getting mad at her isn't working. Let's try to be nice to her. I'll help."

Kathy nodded. "Thanks," she said with a smile. They started up the stairs to Linda's room. "I guess I have been kind of mean to her. I just keep remembering all those awful things she's done in the past. I don't trust her."

Linda nodded as she opened the door to her bedroom. The signs were heaped in a corner. Linda held up the top poster and gasped. It was one she'd decorated with a cute little pony pulling a cart. Now all she could see was a wheel of the cart. The rest of the picture had been splashed with red paint.

Kathy rushed up beside her. "Oh, no!" she cried. "Carly's done it again!"

5 ♦♦♦♦

"That does it," Kathy fumed. "I don't care what Bob and Larry think. I'm going to tell off my dear little cousin."

"Kathy, wait!" Linda whirled around, knocking over the stack of signs. But Kathy had already gone. Linda could hear her cowboy boots clattering down the stairs. Sighing, she bent down to restack the signs. As she shuffled them into a pile her eyes suddenly widened. The top poster was the only one that was ruined. The other signs were better! Carly, or someone else, had changed "Pony Place" to "Pony Palace," just by adding an *a*. And castles, fairies, and winged horses had been added to the other drawings.

Linda sat back on her heels. Not only were the new drawings good, but the new name was really catchy. The Pony Palace. It was great! They could decorate the riding area at the fair like an enchanted kingdom. The kids would love it.

Linda had to catch Kathy. If Kathy chewed Carly out, she'd never live it down.

Linda ran down the stairs and burst into the family room. No one was in sight. Where had they gone?

Laughter came from outside. She peered out the window and saw Bob and Larry leading Nacho out of the barn. Carly was waiting for them in the driveway, holding tightly onto Jackie's hand. Marni was kneeling next to her, as if trying to convince Carly not to be afraid.

Out of the corner of her eye Linda saw Kathy charging from the house.

"Kathy!" she hollered through the closed window. Kathy didn't stop. Linda banged on the glass. She had to get Kathy's attention before she made a giant fool of herself in front of everybody.

Banging louder, Linda screamed at the top of her lungs. Kathy hesitated, turning in the direction of the noise. Linda threw open the window.

"Come quick," Linda called. "It's an emergency!"

At the word "emergency" Kathy froze. She turned and ran into the house. Linda met her in the kitchen.

"What's wrong?" Kathy clutched Linda's hand. "Are you all right?"

"I'm fine! But you were about to get clobbered." Linda shut the door. She glanced outside, but no one had heard her.

"You're fine? You scared me to death!"

"Come here and I'll show you." Linda led Kathy upstairs. "Look." Kneeling on the floor, she separated the pictures.

Kathy stared at them with a puzzled expression. "Who did this? Carly?"

Linda shrugged. "I guess."

"They're . . . they're . . . great!"

"I know. That's why I had to keep you from yelling at her."

"Thanks. I really owe you one." Kathy studied the posters closely. "I didn't know Carly could draw this well."

"There's probably lots of things you don't know about your cousin," Linda said as she stacked the pictures back up.

"Maybe. Anyway, I better go thank her. Maybe I could even help her get on Nacho."

Kathy and Linda hurried outside. Bob, Larry, and Nacho were nowhere in sight. Carly, Marni, and Jackie were walking slowly toward the house. Carly's shoulders were slumped.

"What happened?" Kathy rushed toward them.

Carly glanced at Kathy and began to cry. "I tried, really I did," she wailed. Jackie put her arm protectively around the girl's quaking shoulders.

"She did, too," Marni explained. "But when she reached up to pat Nacho, he bit her."

"Nacho?" Linda exclaimed in disbelief. "He wouldn't hurt a flea."

"I didn't really see it," Jackie explained. "But I don't think he was trying to be mean or anything."

"Yes he was!" Carly sobbed. "He sank his teeth right into my arm."

"Let me see." Linda took Carly's arm. She and Kathy looked it over and exchanged glances. There wasn't a mark on the little girl's arm.

"I don't see a thing," Kathy said. "Are you sure about Nacho?" she asked Carly.

Her cousin began to wail again. "You don't believe *anything* I say." She yanked her arm from Linda's grasp.

"It's not that," Linda said quickly. "It's just that Nacho's never bitten anyone before."

Jackie crouched down and hugged Carly. "Quit grilling her like she's a criminal." She gave Kathy and Linda accusing looks. "Poor kid. She was trying to be so brave. Shame on Nacho."

Linda and Kathy stared at Jackie. Hadn't Jackie heard anything they'd said? How could she believe Carly when the evidence showed she was lying—or at least stretching the truth?

Marni bent down and hugged Carly, too. Linda saw Kathy roll her eyes. And no wonder. The two of them were cooing over Carly just as Aunt Betty did.

Kathy sighed in defeat. Carly had won again.

"Don't cry, Carly. We believe you." Kathy glanced guiltily at Linda. "And, hey—you did a *great* job on the posters and signs. Wait until you see them, Marni."

"What are you talking about?"

"Carly drew castles and fairies and elves on the signs. Then she changed the name to the Pony Palace. Don't you love it?"

Marni nodded. "Yeah. What a great idea!"

Kathy and Marni beamed at Carly, who was suddenly grinning from ear to ear. Her tears had magically disappeared.

Now it was Linda's turn to frown. Kathy might have forgiven her cousin, but Linda had not. She didn't like Carly accusing Nacho of misbehaving when he hadn't.

"Don't overdo it," she whispered to Kathy. But her

friend was so busy exclaiming over Carly, she didn't hear Linda's warning.

Sunday night Bronco dropped Linda off at the Highway House. As a special treat, Mr. and Mrs. Hamilton were taking Linda, Carly, and Kathy to the movie *Hot Kids*. For weeks Linda had been dying to see it.

When Bronco stopped the jeep Linda kissed him goodbye, then jumped from the vehicle and ran up the steps into the restaurant. Kathy met her at the door. Before Linda could say a word Kathy grabbed her elbow and whisked her up the stairs to the private rooms where the Hamiltons lived.

Kathy's bedroom was down a long hall. Kathy put a finger to her lips, and the two girls tiptoed silently past the other doors and into her room. Then Kathy shut the door and collapsed on the bed in a fit of silent giggling.

"What's the big secret?" Linda asked, stretching out beside her.

"Your trick worked great. *Too* great." Kathy rolled her eyes. "Carly's been tagging after me like a puppy. She really thinks I like her." She sat up. "She's been telling everyone how stupid our old posters were and how *she* made them better! I was dying to tell her off.

But she hasn't done anything nasty since then. Being nice is almost worth it."

"I didn't think your truce with Carly would last this long."

"Neither did I. Hey!" Kathy reached out and touched the necklace around Linda's neck. "You're wearing your friendship heart. Let me get my half." Kathy jumped off the bed and began looking in a jewel box on top of her dresser.

"That's funny. I can't find it." Kathy put her hands on her hips and frowned. "I keep all my jewelry in here."

"When did you wear it last?" Linda asked.

"Last week. You know, when we both slept over at Marni's."

"Maybe you left it there."

"No." Kathy rummaged through her backpack. Then she checked the top drawer of her dresser. "I'm positive I brought it home."

Linda got off the bed and began hunting on the bedside table.

"Linda! Kathy!" Mrs. Hamilton's voice called from downstairs. "Time to go!"

"Just a minute!" Kathy yelled back. "It makes me mad when I can't find stuff," she said to Linda, who was busy searching under the bed.

"I know what you mean." Linda sneezed. "Nothing under here but dust."

"Girls!" Mr. Hamilton boomed. "If you don't hurry, we'll be late."

"Phooey. I'll look for it later." Kathy opened the door, and they trooped down the hall. At the bottom of the stairs Carly stood between Kathy's mother and father with a sly grin on her face.

"What's the big rush?" Kathy asked as Carly went with Mr. Hamilton to get the car. "I thought the movie didn't start till seven thirty."

"We're going to see *Snow White* instead," Mrs. Hamilton explained. There was a note of apology in her voice.

"Snow White!"

"I was afraid the other movie might be a little too scary for Carly."

"Hot Kids isn't scary at all!" Kathy cried.

Mrs. Hamilton ushered the girls out the door. "Well, it is pretty grown-up. You know what I mean. Anyway, Carly wants to see *Snow White* more, so end of discussion."

Kathy's face had a look that could kill. Linda wanted to strangle Carly, too. It was the last weekend *Hot Kids* was playing.

"Why don't you drop Linda and me off at the other

theater?" Kathy suggested as they jumped into the back of the car.

"Sorry." Mr. Hamilton's voice was firm. "This is a family outing. Besides"—he turned and looked at them meaningfully—"if I can watch *Snow White,* you girls can, too."

Kathy slumped against the seat. She knew not to argue with her dad. Linda squeezed her hand, trying to signal that everything was okay.

Carly sat in the front seat, chattering the whole way to the theater. While she was jabbering on and on about how wonderful the new posters were, Kathy crossed her eyes and made a face as if she'd eaten a lemon. It was all Linda could do to keep from laughing out loud.

When they got to the movie Mr. Hamilton gave them extra money for treats.

"He's trying to bribe us," Kathy whispered. "I've only seen *Snow White* about twenty times."

"I've seen it at least twenty-one times," Linda whispered back.

They bought huge sodas, popcorn, and candy, then made their way down the dark aisle. Kathy ended up beside Carly. Her cousin was daintily eating a handful of popcorn.

With a grin Kathy opened her box of candy,

popped a fistful into her mouth, and began to chew like a cow—loudly.

Linda tried not to giggle. She'd never seen Kathy act so silly—especially when her parents were around. But they didn't even notice—the theater was filled with noisy little kids.

The lights dimmed, and Linda turned her attention to the picture. A cartoon flashed on the screen. In the middle of a chase scene Linda felt an elbow dig into her side.

Kathy was motioning for Linda to look at Carly. Linda leaned forward and peered. Carly was staring at the screen as if hypnotized. She really looked like a sweet, innocent child. Maybe she and Kathy would finally get along.

Then Linda looked closer. With a gasp she realized what Kathy had wanted her to look at. Dangling from a chain around Carly's neck was half of a gold heart. Carly was wearing Kathy's necklace.

6 ♦♦♦♦

Linda stared at the necklace. When she looked back at Kathy, Kathy looked furious. Carly turned and saw them staring at her.

"Give that to me!" Kathy whispered sharply, lunging forward. "It's mine."

Carly's fingers curled around the heart, clutching it tightly.

"It is not! I found it," Carly answered.

"You did not. You took it from my room." Kathy's voice rose. She grabbed hold of Carly's hand and tried to pry her clenched fingers from the necklace.

"What is going on?" Mrs. Hamilton sat forward.

Carly leaned against Mrs. Hamilton. Kathy let go of the heart.

"She took my necklace," Kathy said.

"It's mine!" Carly cried.

"Kathy! Act your age!" Mrs. Hamilton frowned.

"But she took it—" Kathy began.

"I don't care. This isn't the place to discuss it. You can wait until the movie's over."

For a second Kathy glared at Carly. Then she slouched down into her seat and stuffed handful after handful of popcorn into her mouth.

With a sigh Linda sat back in her seat. It was going to be a very long movie.

When the bus dropped Linda off at school the next morning, she spied Kathy walking up the sidewalk. She waved and ran after her friend. She was dying to find out what had happened with the necklace.

"I don't want to talk about it." Kathy set her mouth tight. Abruptly she swung her backpack off her shoulder and began rummaging through it.

Linda could tell by the way her friend was acting that things hadn't gotten any better between her and Carly. She decided to drop the subject.

"Did you bring those cardboard boxes we need to make the castle?" Linda asked. The three girls were meeting at Marni's house after school to work on props for the fair. They'd decided a ticket booth made up to look like a castle would really enhance the Pony Palace.

"No," Kathy answered. "My mom's dropping them off. I won't be there."

"Why not?"

"Why do you think?" Kathy shoved some papers into her backpack and swung it over her shoulder.

"You're not grounded or anything, are you?" Linda asked, frowning.

"Worse than that. They're making me take Carly over to the Simpsons' house to play with Jessica. Can you believe it?"

"Didn't you tell your mom—" Linda began, but she stopped when Kathy shot her an impatient look.

"Of course I told her how important this booth for the fair is. But she thinks that if Carly meets someone her own age, maybe she won't be so lonely."

"Well, that does make sense, I guess," Linda said slowly.

"Sure. Only no matter what, I'm still stuck with her."

The bell rang, and the two girls began walking into the school. Linda wanted to say something that would make Kathy feel better, but she didn't know what. It seemed that no matter how hard they all tried, Carly was still ruining their plans.

Later, at Marni's house, Linda discussed the situation with Marni and her younger sister, Amy. The three girls were out in the backyard, cutting and taping cardboard boxes into what they hoped was the shape of a castle.

"Carly doesn't sound that bad to me," Amy said as she sketched out the turrets of a tower.

"I guess you had to be there," Marni told her.

"Yeah," Linda said. She was standing in the middle of a carton. "Kathy's cousin is in the big league of brats."

"I just wish we could do something to help," Marni said.

"Me, too." Linda nodded. "But Kathy doesn't even like to talk about it now. And when she does, she almost bites your head off." She sighed. "I think Kathy's going to have to work this one out on her own."

It wasn't until Friday afternoon that Linda mentioned Carly's name again. She and Kathy were walking down the hall after school. The school bus was waiting, so she had to talk fast.

"I wanted to ask you over tomorrow night—you know, after the fair. I don't know what to do about Carly, though. I mean, can you come without her?"

"Oh, she'll have to come, all right." Kathy let out a puff of air. "She has to ruin everything."

Linda stopped. In the noisy hall kids streamed past, bumping and jostling against her.

"Do you want to talk about it?"

Kathy shrugged. "There's nothing to talk about. My mom said that Carly probably wants my attention. That's why she took the necklace. She wore it for two whole days!" Kathy added angrily. "Can you believe it? That's our special necklace we got together. I kept waiting for Carly to drop it down the toilet or something. Finally my mom made her give it back."

"I wonder if it's true." Linda looked thoughtful as she followed the last group of kids to the bus. "Maybe she does want your attention. You're fun to be with."

Kathy shrugged. "Who knows? But the more she hangs around, the bigger pain she is—asking stupid questions, whining that she's bored. I wish her mom and dad would get back."

Linda glanced up. Kids were hurrying to her bus. "Well, maybe you should try again to treat her like a friend. Pretend she's me."

"You sound like my mom." Kathy snorted. "Besides, I already tried. It's Carly who's not trying." Her voice grew louder. "She's so spoiled. She doesn't care about anybody but herself."

Linda started to board her bus. "Just try again," Linda called. Kathy was being pretty stubborn. She

57

didn't see that she was part of the problem, too. "After all, you wouldn't want someone calling *you* a spoiled brat."

But Kathy didn't turn around. Linda could tell by the set of her shoulders that Kathy was mad at her now. For a second Linda thought about getting off the bus, but it was too late. The bus pulled away.

The bus left her off at the end of Rancho del Sol's drive. Linda jogged toward the house, but instead of going right in, she ran to the barn to see Amber. For the last week she'd spent every afternoon finishing up the cardboard castle for the pony ring. She hadn't had much time to pay attention to her horse.

Amber was standing in the cool barn, out of the hot southern California sun. When she saw Linda she turned in her stall and stuck her head over the door.

"Hey, girl, did you miss me?" Linda whispered as she stroked the mare's golden neck. "I missed you this week. But I've been too busy with the fair to ride."

Amber blew softly on Linda's cheek, then moved away to stand in the corner.

She must be mad, Linda thought. Amber had never done that before. She would make it up to her with a good brushing and a long ride. But first she needed to change her clothes and get a snack.

She was turning to go when she noticed grain in the bottom of Amber's feed bucket. Frowning, Linda checked it. Sometimes, if the bucket was dirty, Amber wouldn't finish her morning grain. But the sweet feed smelled delicious, and the bucket was clean.

Feeling worried, Linda opened the door and went into the stall. She placed her hand on Amber's forehead, feeling to see if she had a temperature, but Amber was cool to her touch.

Amber nudged her gently with her nose, then hung her head. Linda shut the stall door and left the stable. Mac's jeep was parked outside, and she could hear his voice coming from the cattle barn.

"Hey! School over already?" Mac straightened as Linda bounded into the barn. He tilted back his cowboy hat and wiped his forehead with a red handkerchief. He'd been tossing hay bales into the loft, and his face was wet with sweat.

"I'm worried about Amber. She didn't finish her grain," Linda explained.

He nodded. "Yeah, I noticed. She didn't attack her feed like she usually does."

"She's not feeling right. I can tell."

"Well, it's probably nothing," Mac said. "Except for that little bit of rain last week, it's been real hot and dry. If she's not better tomorrow morning, I'll give her a good checkup. Until then, no riding. Just in case," he added quickly.

Linda nodded with relief. She felt better already. Mac was great with horses. She knew, too, that if Mac was worried, he'd call Dr. Burnside, the veterinarian. Either way, Amber would be in the best of hands.

Linda went back to the barn. She scooped up a handful of feed and offered it to Amber. The palomino took it from her and crunched it eagerly. Maybe Mac was right. Maybe the dry, dusty weather was all that was making Amber listless.

Linda ran down the drive, through the Dutch door, and into the kitchen. "Hi! I'm home!" She grabbed a handful of oatmeal cookies from a batch that was cooling on the counter.

"In here," Doña called from the ranch's office.

As Linda went in Doña sat back in her desk chair and took off her glasses. Linda sat down on the armrest and peered at the computer screen.

"Does that stuff make sense?" she asked.

"Only if you understand bookkeeping." Doña smiled.

"Well, I might understand that better than I understand people." Linda sighed. She popped a cookie into her mouth and began munching.

"What people don't you understand?" Doña leaned forward.

"Kathy—and her bratty cousin," Linda said. "Ever since Carly's been here Kathy's acted like a different person. She moped around all week. When I tried to talk to her she just about bit my head off."

"Did you ask her to spend the night Saturday?" Doña asked. "Maybe she'll relax once the fair is over."

Linda nodded. "She might get excited about sleeping over."

Doña patted Linda's arm. "I bet if you call Kathy and ask her again, she'll come."

"Which means Carly has to come, too. Which means Kathy will spend the whole night sulking."

"Umm. I see your problem." Suddenly Doña squeezed Linda's hand. "I know. We'll plan something so exciting to do that Kathy and Carly won't have time to get on each other's nerves."

"Good idea, Doña!" Linda gave her a huge hug. Smiling happily, she bit into another cookie. Then her smile faded. "That still leaves a big problem."

"What's that?" Doña put on her glasses and began studying the computer screen.

"What can we do that's so exciting that Kathy and Carly will forget about each other?"

61

"Oh, you leave that up to Bronco and me." Doña's eyes twinkled. "We'll think of something."

"Okay. Thanks." Linda hugged her grandmother again, then headed for the phone in the family room. She plopped into Bronco's comfortable leather chair and dialed the Hamiltons' number.

Kathy answered on the first ring.

"Hi! It's me," Linda said. "I just wanted to remind you that we're meeting at the pony ring first thing tomorrow morning. I'll practically be getting up at dawn to help Bronco load the ponies," she added with a groan.

"I'll see you over there," Kathy replied. "Mom said she'd help me take all the signs and stuff over real early."

Linda couldn't tell if Kathy was still mad at her. As they chatted on about the fair, though, she finally decided everything was okay.

"So can you stay over tomorrow night?" Linda asked.

"Sure, I'm coming," Kathy said. "And Carly is, too. We should have lots of fun." She sounded so cheerful that Linda wondered what was going on.

There was a pause on the other end of the wire. Then Kathy lowered her voice. "Good, the little snoop is gone. What I really meant was that Carly says she's mad at me because I've been mean to her all week—which I haven't—and that she's not going to help us at the fair tomorrow at all. That means we'd better keep a close eye on Miss Sneaky. I have a feeling she's planning something to get me in really *big* trouble!''

7 ♦♦♦♦

Linda woke with a sense of excitement. The fair was that day! She dressed and ate breakfast in record time. Only one thing worried her—Amber. She hurried into the barn to find Mac there ahead of her.

"What's Amber's temperature?" Linda asked. Mac was squinting at the thermometer in his hand.

"One hundred degrees. Just what a healthy horse's temperature should be." He gave the long thermometer a shake.

"She doesn't look too good." Linda ran her hand down Amber's silky neck. The palomino shook her head, and her creamy white mane flew in the air.

"At six o'clock in the morning nobody looks too good." Mac chuckled, then gave Linda a reassuring nod. "Don't worry. While you're at the fair today I'll keep a close eye on her."

"Linda!" Bob's voice rang down the aisle of the barn. "Let's go."

Linda handed Amber's lead line to Mac. "I'll call as soon as I can," she said. Giving Amber one last pat, she ran from the stall.

Bronco was in the driver's seat, warming up the pickup. Hooked to the truck was the ranch's six-horse trailer. Linda could hear Nacho's shrill whinny as he called to the horses in the barn. Poor Nacho was all alone in the back of the huge trailer, but as soon as they got to Flying Star Ranch to pick up the other ponies he'd have lots of company.

Linda hopped up front with Bronco and Bob. Larry and two guitars were squashed into the truck's shallow backseat.

"Where's the rest of your gear?" Linda asked.

"Stashed in a trailer stall," Bob answered with a yawn. Behind him Larry was half asleep. His head bobbed on the backseat as the truck bounced down the drive.

"Is there enough room for Glen Manlon's ponies?" Linda asked Bronco.

He laughed. "We could fit about twenty of those pint-sized critters back there."

As they drove along Bob began to hum quietly.

Linda listened for a minute. It helped take her mind

off Amber. "That sounds like one of the songs Jackie wrote."

Bob nodded and started to sing. When he hit a high note his voice was scratchy and shrill.

"Only you don't sound much like Jackie," Linda added, plugging her ears. "Lucky Amber isn't with us, or she'd really get sick."

Bob just sang louder. Larry snorted and snapped awake. "What's all that racket? Did we have an accident?" he asked in a dazed voice.

Linda and Bronco burst out laughing.

"Really funny, Larry," Bob said, reaching back and punching his friend in the arm.

"How is Amber, by the way?" Bronco asked.

Linda shrugged. "She didn't have a temperature this morning."

Her grandfather patted her knee. "Don't worry. I'll be driving back from the fair early. I'll help keep an eye on her."

"Thanks." Still, Linda couldn't help wonder what was wrong with Amber. The palomino was never sick. Linda just hoped everything would be okay.

They pulled into the driveway of the Flying Star Ranch. Glen Manlon waved from the doorway of the barn. Bronco parked the trailer, and Linda slid out.

Glen was leading a shaggy pinto pony from the barn. Linda recognized the horse.

"Hi, Polka Dot," she crooned, taking the rope from Glen while he went back to get two other ponies.

Bronco and Bob opened the back of the trailer, and Nacho gave a loud squeal of delight. Linda led Polka Dot up the ramp and backed him into the stall next to Nacho. Then, one by one, they loaded the rest of the ponies. When they were through Linda rode with Glen Manlon in his jeep, and he gave her last-minute instructions.

"Since the fair lasts most of the day, the ponies will have to be rested about every hour. That means you should give rides in shifts. Use three of the ponies while the others graze."

Linda nodded. Mr. Manlon had helped them rope off a riding area and a grazing area at the fairgrounds.

"You and your friends will have to pay close attention."

"We will," Linda promised. "Don't worry—the ponies will be fine."

The Lockwood Fairgrounds were decorated with booths and banners. Bronco and Mr. Manlon drove right up to the pony ride area.

"Linda—hi! Over here!"

Kathy ran over and helped Linda unload the saddles and bridles from the jeep.

"The place still looks great!" Linda said. She looked around at the signs and posters they had set up after school that week. The castle was standing at the entrance to the roped-off area. Just as Linda had thought, it really added a lot of pizzazz. They had set up a chair and a ticket box behind the castle.

Linda glanced around and lowered her voice to a whisper. "Where's Carly?"

Kathy nodded toward a tree. Carly was stretched out in the shade, pretending to read a book.

"She isn't lifting a finger to help," Kathy said. "But then, she isn't wrecking anything, either."

"Let's leave her alone and keep our fingers crossed," Linda said. "Maybe the whole day will go easy."

"We need a hand over here, girls!" Bronco called. He'd stretched a rope between two trees in the middle of the grazing ring. Glen Manlon was unloading the ponies. Kathy helped him while Linda took hold of each pony. She led them to the taut rope, tying them to it with the lead line.

When all the ponies were secured Bronco drove off

with Bob and Larry and their band equipment. Then, satisfied that the girls knew what they were doing, Glen Manlon left, too.

As his jeep disappeared from the fairgrounds Linda had a sinking feeling in her stomach. What if something *did* go wrong? Being in charge of six ponies was a lot of responsibility.

But she soon forgot her worries as Marni joined them and the three girls brushed and saddled Nacho, Polka Dot, Lollipop, Bandit, Sunshine, and Twinkle. Linda had forgotten about Carly until she felt her hanging around while she braided a ribbon into Nacho's tail.

"Gee, that looks neat," Carly said.

"Would you like to help? I'll show you how."

Carly wrinkled her nose, then hesitantly stepped forward, her eye on Nacho.

"He won't hurt you," Linda assured her.

"Well, I am getting kind of bored."

"Here. You hold two hunks of his hair in your right hand. Take the ribbon in your left, then crisscross them, just like you were braiding your own hair."

"I can do that!" Carly grasped Nacho's tail. Suddenly the little Shetland pony stamped his back hoof at a fly.

With a shrill cry Carly jumped sideways. She looked down and began to scream so loud, Linda was sure they could hear it all over the fairgrounds.

Kathy and Marni rushed over. "What's wrong? What happened?" they both exclaimed.

Flicking his ears, Nacho turned and stared at them as if wondering what all the excitement was about.

"That pony kicked me!" Carly cried. "Right into this." She pointed at her sneakers. "Oh, yuck! My new shoes are ruined!" She started to cry.

Kathy gave Linda a confused look.

"Nacho didn't kick her. He stamped his foot, and she slipped—well, she stepped in manure." Linda tried to be serious, but the sight of Carly crying over horse manure was too much. Linda started to laugh, and Marni and Kathy joined in. Instantly Carly stopped crying. Her mouth dropped open, and she stared at the three girls in disbelief.

"It's not funny! Stop laughing!" she demanded.

Kathy gasped between chuckles. "You're acting like it's some kind of poison."

"Maybe the evil wizard who lives in our castle put it there," Marni said to Carly in a spooky voice.

Carly gave the girls a really dirty look, then turned and stomped back to her tree.

"We'd better say something nice to her," Linda said. "She *was* trying to help."

"Oh, leave her alone," Kathy said. "Let her sulk. Any other kid would've thought it was funny."

"Look, here comes Ms. Gifford." Marni pointed. "Let's meet her at the castle."

Kathy and Marni excitedly took off. Linda finished Nacho's tail, checked to make sure the ponies were secure, then hurried to the castle at the entrance to the riding ring.

"I'm impressed," Ms. Gifford was saying. "You girls really worked hard."

"When are the kids from the special class coming?" Marni asked. They'd planned to give them free rides before the fair opened officially.

Ms. Gifford checked her watch. "In about half an hour. I'll be back with Kelly. She promised to come so there will be plenty of help."

"I can't wait. It'll be so much fun!" Kathy cried.

"I'm glad we're doing them first," Linda added. "Because I have a feeling that by the time the fair closes we're going to be too tired to move."

Just then Linda felt a strange nibble behind her. She whirled. Nacho was nuzzling her back pocket, searching for carrots.

"Nacho! What—" She looked up. Lollipop was ambling toward the carnival games, and Bandit was grazing by the side of the drive.

Linda grabbed Kathy's arm and twirled her around. "The ponies!" she cried. "They're loose!"

8 ◆◆◆◆

Linda grabbed Nacho's dangling lead line. She thrust it into Marni's hand. "Here. Hold him while I get Polka Dot!" The pinto was walking toward the parking lot. She had to get him before he reached the road.

Linda dashed after him. "Hey, guy, hey, buddy, it's me," she crooned when she caught up to him. She stretched out her hand as if she had a treat. Ears pricked, Polka Dot halted. He reached out his head and snuffled curiously at her fingers. Linda scooped up the lead line.

She let out a sigh of relief. "Sorry, Polka Dot. I was just pretending I had a treat," she told the pinto as she rumpled his mane. "I didn't want you to get hit by a car."

Grasping the lead line firmly, she turned to see

where the rest of the ponies were. Marni had hold of Nacho and Bandit, and Ms. Gifford was leading Lollipop. The teacher had a disapproving look on her face.

Linda clucked to Polka Dot and led him toward the grazing corral. Twinkle and Sunshine were already in the ring, cropping grass. As Linda drew closer she could see that they were still tied to the picket line. The problem was that one end of the rope had fallen down. The four "runaway" ponies had slipped their lead lines right off the end.

Linda frowned as she studied the picket line. Bronco had tied it, and she had just checked it. How had the rope come loose?

"What happened?" Marni asked as they led the escaped ponies into the corral.

Linda shook her head, then stopped and picked up the rope. It wasn't frayed or broken. Someone must have untied it.

"I hope you girls have an explanation for this," Ms. Gifford said in a stern voice.

Marni and Linda exchanged worried glances. If Ms. Gifford was mad enough, she might close down the rides.

"I don't know what happened," Linda finally said. "Bronco tied it, and I—"

A sharp squeal interrupted her. Kathy was marching toward them, towing Carly by the hand.

"This is what happened!" Kathy gave her cousin a push forward. Carly's lips trembled, and she was ready to cry.

"None of that baby stuff," Kathy said sternly. "Just tell the truth."

Carly stared down at her sneakers. "I untied the rope," she said. "But I didn't mean for them to get away. I thought the ponies would stay in their little corral. Honest!"

She stared up at them. Tears glistened in her eyes. For once Linda believed her. Carly was a pest, but Linda didn't think she would hurt the ponies.

"It's good you're not in my class, young lady," Ms. Gifford said. "I'd make you wash blackboards for a month! One of the ponies could have been injured. Do you know that?"

With a loud sniff Carly nodded.

"So instead of blackboards, you have ticket duty for the afternoon," Ms. Gifford continued. "That means you don't leave that castle for a second."

Carly nodded again. Linda thought she saw a look of relief on Carly's face. Maybe Ms. Gifford's punishment was just what Carly needed. It would give her something important to do.

"And as for you girls"—Ms. Gifford turned to Linda, Marni, and Kathy—"I expect everything double-checked for safety."

Linda nodded sheepishly as Ms. Gifford left.

Carly scampered over to the castle and sat on the chair. The others led three ponies back to the corral just as the special kids showed up for their pony rides.

Linda spotted Lisa and brought Sunshine over to her wheelchair. The little palomino nuzzled Lisa's shoulder, and Linda suddenly remembered Amber. In all the confusion she'd forgotten to call home.

Kelly Michaels came up to give Linda a hand with Lisa. As Linda led Lisa and Sunshine around the ring she silently scolded herself. Amber could be really sick, and she wouldn't even know.

"Come one, come all to the Pony Palace!" Kathy's voice broke through Linda's thoughts. Kathy was standing beside the castle. She waved a magic wand and called to the crowd that was streaming into the fairgrounds.

Linda glanced down at her watch. She couldn't believe it! It was time to start selling rides. She'd never be able to call the ranch now.

Kelly lifted Lisa off Sunshine. Already a line of squealing kids and their parents was forming at the entrance to the ring. Marni darted back and forth collecting money, and Carly handed out tickets.

Linda's first customer was a little boy. He rushed into the ring with a cowboy suit on. He ran behind Sunshine and stuck a pretend gun into Linda's ribs.

"Stick 'em up!" he growled. Linda rolled her eyes. She had to do this for eight more hours?

Just then she heard someone call her name. Bob was standing on the other side of the ring.

"Amber's doing okay," he called through cupped hands. "Mac says not to worry!"

Linda gave him the thumbs-up sign. A grin spread across her face, and she felt as if a huge weight had been lifted off her shoulders. With a laugh she reached down and grabbed the little boy under the arms.

"Guess what, pardner," she said as she swung him onto Sunshine's back. "You're under arrest. You just made a big mistake. You stuck up the sheriff!"

Three hours later Linda's legs felt like rubber. They'd made sure to give the ponies a rest but had forgotten all about resting themselves. And the rides were so popular, there was still a line. It seemed to stretch for miles.

Leading Nacho, Marni staggered up to Linda. Her red hair was stuck to her sweaty forehead, and her cheeks were smudged with dirt. Linda didn't dare laugh. She knew she must look just as bad.

"Fifty." Marni gasped as if it was her last breath. "I counted how many times I walked around the ring— it was fifty."

"You're kidding," Linda said. An eager, fresh-faced girl raced over for a ride. With weary arms Linda lifted her into Bandit's saddle. She counted quickly in her head. "That means we've done a total of two hundred laps around this ring."

"Two hundred!" Kathy exclaimed behind them. She was leading a pudgy boy on Nacho. "That must be a world's record. We definitely need a break."

"The Hombres are on at four o'clock," Linda said. "Let's post a sign—rides closed from four to five. Then we'll have time to eat and watch them play."

"Good idea."

Linda held Nacho while Kathy took a marker and scribbled out a sign to hang on the castle.

At four on the dot the girls watered the ponies, tethered them, loosened their saddles, and threw them some hay for dinner. They agreed they couldn't leave the ponies alone, so they drew strands of hay to choose who would stay. Marni lost—she had the first twenty-minute watch.

"Only if you bring me back something to eat," Marni said. She sank onto a bale of hay. "Ah-h-h. Does this ever feel good!"

"Burger and fries okay?" Linda asked.

"Make that *two* burgers, tons of ketchup, double fries, and a giant lemonade."

Linda wrote down the order on a piece of scrap paper. "What do you think Carly will want?" she asked Kathy.

"I don't know. Let me ask her." Kathy turned toward the castle. "Hey, Carly, what do you want for dinner?" she called. There was no answer.

"I don't think she's over there." Linda stood on tiptoes, trying to see over the castle walls.

"Oh, great." Kathy trudged over toward the riding ring. When she got there she yelled back, "She's not here! Where could she have gone?"

"Did you see her?" Linda asked Marni. She'd been the last one out of the ring.

Marni thought for a moment. "She collected the ticket for the last ride. After that"—she shrugged—"I don't remember seeing her."

"I can't believe it!" Kathy stormed over. "She's nowhere around here!"

"Maybe she went to the carnival rides or to get something to eat," Linda suggested.

"That's just super," Kathy said sarcastically. "My mother warned me a hundred times to watch out for Carly. If she gets lost, I'm in big trouble."

Linda could see that Kathy was getting really steamed. Not that she blamed her. They were all too hungry and tired to be worrying about Carly.

"Come on, we'll look for her. Marni will be here in case she comes back." Linda tugged on Kathy's arm.

"Okay," Kathy grumbled as they headed toward the carnival rides. "But we better find her before my parents come by." She shook her head. "I don't even want to *think* about what'll happen then."

"Don't forget my two burgers!" Marni called after them.

Linda and Kathy went to the carnival rides, figuring the bright lights and music had lured Carly away.

Shading her eyes with her hand, Linda scanned the Ferris wheel and the Tilt-a-Whirl. Kathy checked out the rocket and the bumper cars. There was no sign of Carly.

As they walked along Linda could smell hot dogs, tacos, funnel cakes, and candy apples. Her mouth began to water. She fished in her pocket for some change. She stared hungrily toward the Big Burger stand. Kathy touched her arm.

"We'd better keep looking," Kathy said wearily. Reluctantly Linda pocketed the change. She knew Kathy was right, even though her growling stomach was telling her it was time to eat.

They walked down the row of games, asking the kids they knew if they'd seen a nine-year-old girl with long brown hair and freckles like Kathy's. The kids all shook their heads no but promised to keep an eye out. At the end of the row Linda heard a squeal and a splash.

"Hey! There's the dunking booth!" Kathy pulled Linda through the crowd toward a curly-topped redhead. It was Marni's sister Amy, who was taking tickets.

Amy was laughing hysterically as a balding man hoisted himself out of the vat of water. Grumbling good-naturedly, he dried himself off with a towel.

"It's Mr. Herman, the principal!" Linda cried.

Kathy giggled. "Knocking Mr. Herman into the water would be better than dunking Ms. Gifford."

"It only costs fifty cents." Linda decided she couldn't pass it up. She took out two quarters and was just about to hand them to Amy when one of their classmates rushed up.

"I think I saw your cousin," he told Kathy. "The one you're looking for."

"Where?" Kathy clutched Linda's arm excitedly.

"Headed toward the parking lot," the boy told her.

"Let's go!" Kathy grabbed Linda's arm and yanked her from the booth. The money flew out of Linda's fingers, but she couldn't stop, much less see where the coins had fallen.

"What if she gets hit by a car?" Kathy moaned as they charged toward the parking lot.

Linda tripped over a rock and almost fell. "Would you slow down?" Stopping to catch their breath, the girls searched the parking lot.

"She's not here." Kathy turned to Linda with a worried look. "You don't think she would've gotten in a stranger's car, do you?"

Linda sucked in her breath. Her heart began to pound. She knew never to accept rides from strangers, but did Carly? She grabbed Kathy's hand. "We'd better call your parents," she said.

Kathy nodded. She and Linda ran back to the riding ring, which was near a telephone booth.

As they passed the ring Linda caught sight of a little girl sitting on a bale of hay, eating cotton candy as if she didn't have a care in the world. *Carly!*

9 ♦♦♦♦

Linda grabbed Kathy's elbow and pulled her to a stop. "There's Carly!" She pointed toward the corral.

Kathy squinted. Carly looked up and waved cheerfully. Kathy's mouth dropped open. "Why, that little sneak," she said angrily. "We've been chasing all over the place, crazy with worry, and she's—she's—eating cotton candy!"

Just then Marni ran up. "Boy, am I glad I found you guys. Carly's here."

"We know," Kathy said. "And I'm going to strangle her!" Kathy charged toward her cousin. When Carly saw how mad she was, she dropped her cotton candy.

Linda caught up to Kathy before she had a chance to get to Carly. "Wait! We have only fifteen minutes to eat. Then we have to go back to work. Let's not waste time."

"I'm not hungry anymore!" Kathy stared down at Carly with angry eyes. Carly backed up against a tree trunk.

"What's wrong with you?" Carly asked in a squeaky voice.

"What's wrong? We spent our whole break hunting everywhere for you. You shouldn't have disappeared like that."

Carly shrugged. "Sorry. I got hungry."

Now it was Linda's turn to get mad. Carly didn't seem the least bit sorry she'd frightened them. "Because of you, we're starving. Plus we missed seeing the Hombres play."

"You had us scared out of our wits," Kathy added. "We had no idea what happened to you."

"Really? You were worried about me?" Carly looked surprised.

"Hey, guys, if you're going to grab us something to eat, you'd better hurry," Marni interrupted.

Carly jumped up. "Can I come? I'm hungry, too."

Kathy looked at Carly with disbelief. Then she turned on her heel and headed toward the Big Burger booth.

"Come on, Carly." Linda took the younger girl's hand. "I'll treat you. You worked hard selling tickets."

"I've got plenty of money," Carly replied. She snatched her hand from Linda's grasp.

Linda watched Carly run after Kathy. She couldn't figure that kid out. But one thing was for sure. Carly wasn't trying too hard to make friends.

The pony rides had been a big success. But that night, as Bronco drove the girls back to Rancho del Sol, no one said a word about them. Kathy sat in the backseat of the pickup truck with her arms folded. Her face was grim. Carly was curled up silently beside her, hugging a huge teddy bear she'd won at the fair.

They were tired after dropping the ponies off at the Flying Star Ranch. Nacho was alone in the trailer, whinnying for his friends. Linda knew how he felt. Kathy was so quiet, Linda was almost sorry she'd invited her and Carly to spend the night. It wasn't going to be much fun.

"You girls must be tired," Bronco said. "I haven't heard you this quiet since . . ." He scratched his head, pretending to think. "Actually, I don't remember you *ever* being this quiet," he joked.

No one laughed.

"The fair was a big success," he said, trying again. "Everyone was talking about how great the Pony Palace turned out."

Linda sighed. "I know. I'm glad. But do you know how many miles we walked today?"

"I hope you won't be too tired for your surprise," Bronco said with a twinkle in his eyes.

"What surprise?" Kathy piped up from the backseat.

Linda perked up, too. She'd forgotten that Doña and Bronco had cooked up something so Carly and Kathy would forget about their feud.

"You'll find out soon enough," Bronco said as he turned onto the drive leading to the ranch house.

"As soon as I check on Amber," Linda said.

Bronco stopped the pickup and trailer in front of the barn, and they all jumped out. The night was beautiful and crisp, and the stars twinkled brightly in the black sky.

Linda ran around to the back of the trailer. She unlatched the door so Bronco could lead Nacho out. As he walked down the ramp he winked at her and pointed to the big pasture.

Linda turned and noticed a flickering glow that lit up the middle of the field. "A bonfire!" she gasped.

"Look at that!" Kathy came up beside Linda. Her

backpack was slung over one shoulder, and she carried a small suitcase. "Is that the surprise?"

Linda shook her head. "I guess so!"

Doña came down the drive with a picnic basket and a blanket.

"We thought you girls might need a little treat after a long day," she said after greeting Linda's two guests. "How about dinner under the stars?"

"Neat!" Kathy and Linda agreed together. Carly was hanging behind them, still holding the teddy bear.

Doña gave Carly a reassuring smile. "Do roasted hot dogs, corn cooked in the coals, and s'mores sound good to you?" she asked.

Linda held her breath. Carly would probably say she was allergic to corn or afraid of the dark—or something that would ruin the surprise.

But Carly broke into a grin and nodded happily.

Linda gave Doña an extra-big hug. "That sounds great."

"Why don't you help Kathy and Carly get settled in your room, then meet me down there?"

"Kathy can show Carly the way," Linda said in a rushed voice. She was already heading for the barn. "I have to check on Amber."

She ran the rest of the way to Amber's stall. Even though it was late, Mac was by the palomino's side.

87

"How is she?" Linda asked. Dashing into the stall, she threw her arms around Amber's neck and gave her a big hug. "I missed you!"

Amber started to nicker a reply, but instead of her usual clear whinny, out came a cough. Linda leaned back, looking at her in alarm.

"What's wrong?" she asked Mac.

"Upper respiratory infection."

"What?"

"A cold," he added quickly. "At least that's what it looks like now. See, she's got a runny nose, just like a person would have."

"Poor Amber," Linda crooned. "Too bad we can't feed you chicken soup."

"I'm going to put her in a different stall," Mac said. He snapped a lead line onto Amber's halter.

"Why?"

"Because a cold can be really catching. In fact, you'd better wash your hands before you go."

"Okay, but first let me help." Linda unhooked the bucket and feed tub, cleaned them thoroughly, then put them in Amber's new stall.

The palomino was moving in a circle, blowing and snorting at the fresh straw.

"She doesn't like being in a new stall," Linda said.

"Well, she'll just have to get used to it," Mac replied. "Until her nose and cough clear up she'll have to be away from the other horses."

Linda nodded that she understood. Amber stuck her head over the stall door and rested it against her arm.

"I'd stay longer," Linda explained as she stroked Amber's soft nose, "but I have guests. I'll come back later."

With one last pat and a heavy heart Linda left her horse. As she jogged down the drive and into the pasture toward the fire her stomach began to growl. The one Big Burger she'd gulped hadn't been enough to eat.

Kathy was sitting on a hay bale. She leaned toward the fire, intent on the hot dogs she was roasting in the flames.

"Not *too* well done," Linda joked as she sat down beside her friend.

Carly was cuddled next to Doña on the blanket. Linda's grandmother was showing her how to make s'mores.

"First a square of chocolate goes on the graham cracker, then a marshmallow. Would you like to try it?"

Carly shook her head happily. Linda couldn't believe how sweet Carly acted when she got lots of attention.

"Come and get it!" Kathy held up the slightly scorched hot dogs. Linda opened up the buns, and Kathy carefully slid the hot dogs into them.

Using long tongs, Doña pulled the steaming, foil-covered corn from the fire and dropped an ear on everybody's plate.

"Wow, this smells great." Linda squeezed ketchup on her hot dog. "And cooked to perfection, Chef Kathy." Linda loved it when hot dogs were dark brown and slightly crisp on the outside.

"Thanks." Kathy passed a plate to Carly.

Her cousin stared at the hot dog as if it were some strange food from outer space. "Yuck!" She wrinkled her nose and pushed the plate away. "That looks like a big fried worm. My mother never makes me eat hot dogs."

Linda stopped in midbite. A worm? Kathy took back the plate in silence. Linda glanced at Kathy's face. Her mouth was set in a straight line, and her eyes shone brightly. Linda couldn't tell if it was only from the fire or if Carly was making Kathy angry.

"How about corn on the cob?" Doña asked cheerfully as she unwrapped a golden ear.

Carly sniffed. "Too messy. My mother always cuts the corn off for me."

"Oh." This time even Doña was silent for a moment.

"Carly." Kathy stood up so fast she knocked her plate to the ground. Linda caught her hot dog before it rolled into the dirt. "If you don't want anything to eat, why don't you go to bed and—"

"How about a peanut butter and jelly sandwich?" Doña interrupted. Taking Carly by the hand, she helped her up from the blanket. "I'll fix you one in the kitchen."

"Okay. But I only like strawberry jam. And none of that yucky whole wheat bread."

"I'm sure we can find *something* you'll like," Doña said smoothly as she steered Carly away from the fire.

Linda shot her grandmother a grateful look. Slowly Kathy sat back down.

"I was going to say 'Go to bed and never bother me again,'" she told Linda. "Boy, I wish that brat wasn't here."

"She sure can ruin a party," Linda agreed. "But let's forget about her. Isn't the fire great?"

"It's okay," Kathy replied, but her voice had lost its enthusiasm.

Silently the two girls ate their hot dogs. An owl

hooted in a nearby treetop. Then something rustled in the bushes.

Wide-eyed, Linda and Kathy stared at each other in surprise. Then both of them burst out laughing.

"Hey!" Kathy said abruptly. "I've got it!" She turned to Linda with a look of glee. "I know how we can keep Carly off our backs for the rest of the night."

"What are you talking about?" Linda unwrapped an ear of steaming corn.

Kathy grinned. "We'll get Mac to tell Carly one of his scary ghost stories. She'll be so spooked, she'll call my parents to take her back to Highway House—and we'll finally get to be alone!"

10 ◆◆◆◆

"If anything can scare Carly, one of Mac's ghost stories can." Linda shivered even though the fire was blazing hot. "They give *me* goose bumps."

Kathy jumped off the hay bale, twirled in a circle, then did a cartwheel in the grass. "And the neatest part is, I won't get blamed."

Linda frowned. "Your parents might yell at you for letting Carly listen."

"No, they won't. You're supposed to tell spooky stories at sleep-overs."

"Shhh. Here she comes now." Linda grabbed her food again, and Kathy sat down next to her. Doña and Carly walked back into the circle of light to find them busily eating.

Doña was carrying a sandwich on a paper plate. Carly had a plastic bag filled with Luisa's famous oatmeal cookies.

"Look what I have." She held them up.

"Great," Linda said. "But what about the s'mores?"

"Carly decided she likes these better," Doña answered. "But you and Kathy can eat what you want." Doña began to pick up the trash. "Anything else going back to the ranch house? I'm going to leave you all alone for a while."

At the word "alone" Kathy and Linda exchanged knowing glances. Linda had to stifle a giggle.

"Thanks, Doña," Kathy said. "We were going to ask Mac to tell us some ghost stories," she added innocently.

"Oh, that'll be fun," Doña replied. "He was talking to Bronco—I'll send him down."

"Great. Thanks," Kathy said.

"I love ghost stories," Carly piped up from the other side of the fire.

"Good. 'Cause Mac's the ghost story champion of Lockwood. Right, Linda?"

"Right." Linda gulped the last of her hot dog. Then she finished cleaning up while Kathy made the s'mores.

Carly was just polishing off her sandwich when an eerie voice came out of nowhere.

"Good evening, campers—welcome to horrible tales by the fireside."

Linda stared into the dark where the voice was coming from. Even though she knew it was Mac, a shiver raced up her spine.

Mac stepped into the firelight. His cowboy hat was pulled low, casting a spooky shadow on his face.

"Eek!" Carly squealed. She hopped off her blanket and ran toward Linda. With a nervous giggle she plopped down close to Linda's side.

"It's just Mac," Linda explained, trying not to smile.

"I know!" Carly pulled away. "I was just pretending to be scared."

Holding two s'mores, Kathy sat down on the hay bale. Carly was in the middle. Kathy handed one of the gooey treats to Linda.

Mac hunkered down on the blanket. He poked a stick into the fire, then looked up at the girls. His eyes studied their faces. Linda held her breath, waiting for him to begin a story.

"It was many, many years ago, when the pony express came through California, that people first began to tell the story of the Phantom Rider."

"You weren't alive back then," Carly scoffed. "So how'd you hear about it?"

Linda jabbed her elbow into Carly's side. "Shhh. You'll ruin the story."

Mac cocked an eyebrow and continued. "One night I was out on the range, tending my fire, cooking up some beans, when suddenly the sound of a horse's hooves pounded right past my camp."

Mac leapt to his feet and looked into the dark. "I sprang to my feet and stared into the moonlit night. But no one was out there.

"Then a bloodcurdling scream pierced the air. I grabbed my shotgun and ran across the desert toward the sound. My heart was racing a mile a minute."

He paused and stared down at the girls with wide eyes. "But nothing was there."

Slowly he knelt back down next to the fire. Linda glanced at Carly. Her mouth had dropped open.

"It wasn't until I got to town the next day that I found out what it was—the Phantom Rider. Seems I'd camped right in the middle of the old pony express route, and—"

Stopping in midsentence, Mac began to stir the glowing embers with his stick. All three girls leaned forward expectantly.

"And . . ." Kathy prompted.

"His name was Billy Barton, the townspeople said. He was the youngest express rider they'd ever had. Well, one night he never showed up for his eight o'clock pickup, so the people rode out to search for him."

Mac reached up and slid off his cowboy hat. "This is all they ever found."

"His hat?" Carly squeaked.

"Where'd he go?" Linda asked.

"Where was the rest of him?" Kathy chimed in.

Mac shrugged. "Don't know. At first people guessed he'd stolen money and run off—sometimes there was money in the saddlebags.

"But then on dark, quiet nights when they began to hear the screams and the pounding hooves, well"— Mac nodded his head knowingly as he slid his hat back on—"they guessed he'd died running for his life."

"But what was after him?" Kathy asked.

"No one knows. Maybe you girls can figure it out."

"Us?" they all chorused.

"Sure." Mac swept his arm in an arc. "Your fire's right in the middle of young Barton's pony express route. And he should be along *any minute.*"

Carly jumped up with a scream. "Let's get out of here!" She tugged on Linda's arm. "I want to go home!"

Kathy gave Linda a triumphant look. *It worked,* she mouthed.

Linda nodded. Then she looked at Carly. The younger girl was smiling broadly.

"Just kidding," Carly said as she flopped back down. "I wasn't really scared. I love ghost stories. Have you ever heard the one about the man with no arms?"

Mac chuckled and stood up. "That story sounds too spooky for me. You girls are on your own." He waved goodbye and started back toward the ranch house.

"The man with no arms?" Kathy repeated.

Carly nodded. "Yeah. You see, one day this man who was really mean kidnapped this little girl."

Gesturing wildly, she began to tell the most gruesome tale Linda had ever heard.

"That's gross, Carly." Holding her stomach, Kathy stood up. "I think I ate too many hot dogs," she groaned.

"Go on up to the house and ask Doña for something," Linda told her, grateful for the interruption.

She didn't want to hear one more word about a man with no arms. "Carly and I can put out the fire."

Kathy nodded. Her face was pale. Clutching her stomach, she rushed away.

"I wonder what's wrong with her," Carly said.

"We just ate too much and too fast," Linda explained. She poked the fire to make sure the coals were out. Then she picked up the blanket to take back to the house.

Carly just stood there.

"Uh, how about helping me?" Linda suggested.

"Oh, you can get it all," Carly called over her shoulder as she started across the pasture.

For a second Linda fumed. Then she strode after Carly. When she reached the house she put away the blanket, threw the trash in the kitchen disposer, and stuck the leftovers in the refrigerator. Kathy was nowhere in sight. Carly was sitting primly at the kitchen table, munching on another cookie. Linda figured she must have eaten ten already.

"When Kathy comes back, tell her I went in the barn to see Amber," Linda told her.

Carly jumped from the chair. "But you already checked on the stupid horse," she said in a whiny voice. "Why don't we go to bed?"

"Because I happen to be worried about that 'stupid horse,'" Linda snapped. She was beginning to sound just like Kathy, and no wonder. After being with Carly all day, she'd had it with her.

Spinning on her heel, Linda stomped out the kitchen door and down the drive. A second later she heard the sound of running feet. She almost wished it was the ghost of Billy Barton. Anything would be better than Carly.

"Let me come with you," the younger girl said breathlessly when she caught up.

Linda stopped. "Only if you keep out of the way and never call her a stupid horse again."

"I won't," Carly said meekly.

Silently the two girls entered the barn.

Amber's stall door was open, and Linda broke into a run. Mac was in the stall, shaking the thermometer. His eyebrows were knit in a worried scowl.

Linda felt her heart pound. "What's wrong?"

"Her temperature shot up." Mac shook the thermometer again. "One hundred four degrees."

Linda sucked in her breath. "That's not good, is it?"

Mac shook his head. "Nope. And her cough's worse."

As if to demonstrate, Amber gave a hacking

wheeze. It sounded like something was rattling in her throat. Linda threw her arms around the mare's neck. Tears pricked her eyes.

"We better call Dr. Burnside and have her come out first thing in the morning," Mac said solemnly. "We've got one sick horse on our hands."

11 ◆◆◆◆

"I'm not leaving Amber's side," Linda announced to Mac. "If she's that sick, I'll sleep here in the barn. She needs to know someone's looking after her."

"There's nothing you can do," Mac replied. "Tomorrow Dr. Burnside will give Amber an antibiotic to knock out the infection. Until then we can give her fresh water and make sure her nose stays clear."

"I can do that." Linda draped her arm across Amber's withers.

Mac shook his head and chuckled. "I can tell there's no use arguing with you. Go get your stuff. I'll wait with Amber until you're ready."

An indignant voice broke into the conversation. "Does that mean we're going to sleep in the barn? 'Cause if it does, then count me out. I wouldn't sleep out here for a million dollars!"

Mac and Linda whirled around. Carly was standing in the middle of the stall entrance, her hands on her hips. Linda had forgotten all about her.

"That means *I'll* sleep in the barn," Linda told her. "You can do whatever you want."

"Good. Because—because—" For once Carly was at a loss for words. Her face lost its scornful look, and she stared at Amber with a sad expression in her eyes.

Linda was puzzled at the girl's sudden change. She knew Carly was afraid of horses, but that didn't seem to explain her latest behavior. Maybe she was afraid of the dark but was too scared to admit it.

"You and Kathy can stay in my room," she explained a little more gently.

Carly nodded, then turned and ran down the aisle.

"What was that all about?" Mac asked.

Linda shrugged. "Who knows? And who cares?" she added. "I've got more important things to worry about."

She unlatched the lead line from Amber's halter, then watched as the mare moved sluggishly to the opposite end of the stall. Linda's heart flip-flopped, but she told herself everything was going to be okay.

Then she closed the stall door and went into the neighboring stall to survey her sleeping quarters. The straw was deep and fresh. If she threw a sleeping bag on top, it would be as soft as a bed.

Mac was leaning over the wooden partition. "Better than the hard ground on some of our camping trips."

"That's for sure," Linda agreed. "Well, I'll get my stuff." She glanced one more time at Amber.

"Would you quit worrying?" Mac said. "I promise I won't move until you get back."

Linda smiled gratefully. "Thanks. Be right back." She dashed from the barn, running her fastest all the way down the drive.

When she got to the ranch house she told Doña what her plans were. Then, taking the steps in twos, Linda went up to her room to get her sleeping bag. Kathy was already sacked out in Linda's bed, reading a book. Carly was tossing and turning in a sleeping bag on the floor.

"It's about time you got here," Kathy said, sitting up. She shut her book. "Is Amber okay?"

Linda shook her head. "Worse. I'm spending the night with her."

Kathy jumped out of bed. "I'm coming with you."

"Thanks, but you don't have to."

"I want to." Kathy slipped on her jeans and tucked in her nightshirt.

"Would you guys be quiet?" Carly said. "It's bad enough trying to sleep on this hard floor."

"You can have the bed," Linda replied as she stuffed some things into her backpack. "We're sleeping in the barn."

"And leaving me here alone?" Carly sat bolt upright. "No way!"

"Back at the barn you told me you wouldn't sleep there for a million dollars," Linda said in an angry tone. Not only did she not want Carly out there, she was sick and tired of the younger girl changing her tune every two seconds.

"Just stay here," Kathy added. "We don't want you with us, I can tell you that."

"Too bad!" Carly retorted. She unzipped her sleeping bag and stood up. She was wearing frilly baby-doll pajamas. "I'm not staying here by myself." Hugging her arms tightly around herself, she glanced nervously about the room.

Linda sighed impatiently. "Then at least put some clothes on over those pajamas, or you'll freeze." She knew arguing with Carly wouldn't do any good. She just hoped Carly would get sick of the barn and want to come back in later.

"And don't bother us!" Kathy shook a finger in Carly's face as they started to leave. "If Amber's sick, we can't worry about you getting stomped on by cows or bitten by tarantulas."

"Cows? Tarantulas?" Carly's voice quavered, but when the others ignored her and headed out the door she quickly found her shoes and came running after them.

In the family room Linda grabbed a flashlight and a deck of cards. In the kitchen the girls raided the refrigerator and cupboards, filling a bag with cookies, fruit, peanuts, napkins, cups, and a jar of lemonade.

Hearing the commotion, Doña peeked around the door. When she saw the pile of stuff in their arms she had to laugh. "You girls have enough supplies for a week."

"It's going to be a long night." Linda crossed the kitchen to give her grandmother a kiss on the cheek.

"Well, it's almost ten o'clock. I suggest you spread out your sleeping bags and go to sleep—pronto."

"We will," Kathy replied. "Especially Carly. It's way past her bedtime."

"Is not!" Carly said as they turned to go. "My mother lets me go to sleep whenever I want. Sometimes I stay up and watch the late movie. Boy, you should see the gory stuff they show! The other night we saw *The Teenage Mummy*."

As they crunched down the gravel drive Carly was still jabbering away. Linda sighed. Amber wasn't going to get much rest with Miss Chatterbox along. Maybe they should put Carly's sleeping bag in the hayloft.

"Carly, will you shut up?" Kathy said in an exasperated tone, as if she'd read Linda's mind.

"No. Why should I?"

"Because." Kathy stopped suddenly and glared down at her cousin. "If you don't, I'll find the hairiest spider in the barn and put it in your sleeping bag."

Carly's eyes grew wide, and her mouth opened. Linda waited for one of her bratty retorts, but all she said was "Oh."

They continued walking. The night was cool and dark, but the barn lights were warm and inviting. Linda shifted the heavy bag of food. If Carly kept her mouth shut, the night could be fun after all.

Mac had spread a thick layer of fresh straw in the clean stall next to Amber's. He said good night, and the girls laid down their sleeping bags. Carly jumped eagerly into hers.

"This is lots better! That hard old floor in Linda's room was killing me," she announced.

Kathy shot her a look that said *Be quiet!*

"Okay, okay," Carly muttered. Grabbing the jar of peanuts from the bag, she started eating. Linda and Kathy left to check on Amber.

The palomino was standing listlessly in the corner. When she saw Linda her ears flicked forward, but then she coughed, and her nose began to drip.

"I've never seen her this sick," Linda said. She fetched a clean paper towel to wipe Amber's nose.

"Poor Amber." Linda smoothed the mare's silky mane. "All we can do is make sure she has lots of clean water and keep her nose free of this gunky stuff."

"I hope the other horses don't catch her cold."

"Me, too. Mac says it's real contagious. That's why Amber is away from the other horses. We have to wash our hands after touching her, too." She stifled a yawn. "Boy, I sure am tired."

"Let's go to sleep." Kathy yawned.

"No. I'm going to watch Amber all night. I'd never forgive myself if something happened to her."

"I'd stay up with you," Kathy said, "but I've had it. Sorry."

"That's okay," Linda told her. "I know you're beat."

Linda threw the paper towel away, washed her hands, then cleaned and refilled Amber's bucket. Amber was snoozing, standing horse-style in the corner, and Linda didn't want to disturb her.

With a gentle pat she left the palomino and went into the other stall. Kathy was sprawled facedown in her sleeping bag, already sound asleep. Carly was curled next to her in a tight ball, the open jar of peanuts propped against her leg.

Linda gazed at Carly. Her rosebud mouth was slightly open, and her hair fell across her cheek. It was hard to believe that anyone who looked so angelic could be such a big pain.

Rummaging through the food, Linda pulled out an apple and a cookie. She sat cross-legged on her sleeping bag and bit into the cookie. Not that she was really hungry—she was too tired even to think about food. Maybe she should just lie down for a second. Stretching out, Linda settled on the soft nest of straw. She yawned. Boy, did the straw feel good.

Linda woke to the sound of crying. Sitting up, she blinked sleepily. For a second she couldn't remember where she was. Then the sight of Kathy sleeping peacefully next to her reminded her she was in the barn because of Amber.

Amber! Linda glanced down at her watch. It was after six o'clock in the morning. She'd slept all night.

She scrambled to her feet. Again she heard crying. Then she noticed Carly wasn't in her sleeping bag. Linda looked over the partition that separated the two stalls.

Amber was lying down. Her legs were tucked underneath her, and her nose rested in the hay. Carly was sitting next to her in the straw. She was curled into the circle of Amber's neck, her head resting on the mare's mane. Linda could see tears streaming down the young girl's face.

"Carly! Are you all right? Is Amber all right?" Linda asked in a hoarse whisper as she rushed into Amber's stall.

Startled, Carly hastily wiped her tears. She jumped up. "Yes. I mean, I think so."

Linda knelt and checked Amber. Her nose was clean, and her bucket had fresh water. Linda patted her neck, and Amber tossed her head, but her brown eyes still didn't have their old spark.

"Did you take care of Amber all the time I was asleep?" she asked Carly.

Carly nodded. Her eyes were brimming with tears.

"You did great. I can't believe it," she said. Carly began crying harder.

Linda was confused. "I don't get it. Why are you still crying?"

"Because." Carly sniffed, then began to wail. "She's going to need an operation!"

12 ◆◆◆◆

"An operation!" Linda jumped to her feet. At her cry Amber slowly gathered her legs underneath her and heaved herself upright. Linda pushed Carly into the barn aisle. She took Carly's shoulders and gave her a shake.

"What are you talking about? Did Mac look at Amber while I was asleep? Did he tell you she needed an operation?" Linda was frantic. She couldn't believe she'd slept through something so important.

Carly shook her head. "Not *Amber*. My mother."

Linda stepped back. Now she was really confused. How had Kathy's aunt Betty gotten into the conversation?

Carly began to weep fresh tears. Linda suddenly understood what she was talking about.

"Your *mother* needs an operation?" Carly nodded. "But I thought she was on a cruise to the Bahamas."

"That's what my parents told me. They didn't want me to know she had to go to the hospital. They lied," Carly added angrily.

"How did you find out?"

"I was listening at the door before they left. They were talking to Kathy's mom and dad. Everyone knew about the operation but me. They thought I was too little to know about it."

"What's going on?" a sleepy voice asked from the other stall.

Linda and Carly both turned to see Kathy in the doorway of the other stall, rubbing her eyes.

Linda glanced down at Carly. Now she understood why Carly had been such a brat all week. She was worried sick about her mother, yet she couldn't talk to Mr. or Mrs. Hamilton because she wasn't supposed to know about the operation.

"I was just telling Carly what a great job she did nursing Amber," Linda said quickly.

"Carly?" Kathy looked skeptical. "But you hate horses," she said to her cousin.

Carly dabbed her tears with her flannel shirt. "Well, you guys were sound asleep, and Amber started coughing, and she knocked over her bucket, and I felt so sorry for her, and . . . oh, Linda!'' She hurled herself at Linda, burying her head in her stomach.

"What's going on?'' Kathy asked. "Is Amber worse?''

"Carly, either *you* tell Kathy, or let *me* tell her,'' Linda said. Without looking up, Carly nodded.

"Tell me what?'' Kathy was even more confused.

"Your aunt Betty is not on a cruise,'' Linda explained. "She's in the hospital having an operation.''

"What?''

"They pretended she was going to the Bahamas so Carly wouldn't worry.''

"How'd Carly find—never mind. I'm sure it has something to do with listening at doors.'' Kathy put her hands on her hips. She had a thoughtful expression on her face. "No wonder Carly's been so upset. I can't believe my mom and dad agreed not to tell her. I'm going to call them right now.''

Linda nodded. Carly's parents probably thought they were doing the right thing by not telling their daughter the truth, but she agreed with Kathy—Carly needed to know.

Kathy slipped on her sneakers and jogged down the barn aisle. It was beginning to get light outside, and Linda could hear the sounds of slamming doors. That meant Mac would soon be up.

Amber snorted gently in her stall. She didn't seem any better, but thanks to Carly, she wasn't any worse.

Cheerful whistling broke into Linda's thoughts as Mac rounded the corner.

"Morning," he greeted them. "You girls are up early." He peered into the stall. "How's your patient?"

"She's okay—thanks to Nurse Carly." Linda gave Carly a squeeze. The younger girl rubbed her eyes sleepily. Linda knew she must have had a hard night—worrying about her mother and Amber, too.

"Dr. Burnside should be here any minute," Mac said as he walked into the stall. "She said we were first on her morning rounds."

"Why don't you go back to the house and get some sleep?" Linda told Carly.

"No way!" Carly protested. "I want to be here when the doctor checks Amber. I hope she's going to be all right."

"That sounds like the doc's truck now." Mac strode down the aisle to greet the veterinarian.

Linda and Carly stayed by Amber. Carly was still holding Linda tight around the waist. Even though Linda was eager to rush from the barn and talk to Dr.

Burnside, she knew Carly needed her attention even more.

"I hear you've got a sick horse," Virginia Burnside boomed as she strode toward the two girls. Without another word she went into Amber's stall. "Not that I don't trust Mac's diagnosis." She winked at Linda.

Linda gently disengaged Carly's arms from around her waist. "I've got to hold Amber," she explained. Luckily, at the same time Kathy jogged back into the barn.

Carly started weeping again. The two cousins hugged each other, then stood outside the stall to watch the veterinarian.

Linda slipped a halter on Amber and held her while the doctor took the horse's temperature and checked her nose for mucus.

"Somebody did a good job of doctoring her last night," the vet said.

Linda smiled at Carly, and the younger girl's face broke into a pleased grin.

"Yes, it's just what I thought." Dr. Burnside bent down and took a huge syringe from her bag. "Equine influenza. Probably picked it up at one of the horse shows you went to. It's been traveling around the county."

She jabbed the needle into Amber's neck, and

Linda winced at the same time. Amber didn't move a muscle.

"Give this to her for five more days," the doctor said, handing Mac a bottle of antibiotic. "Keep up the good care, and she'll be as good as new." Dr. Burnside packed up her things, and Mac escorted her from the barn.

"Thank you!" Linda called. Then she gave Amber a big hug of relief. Everything was going to be okay. "Equine influenza" sounded terrible, but as Mac had said, it was only a bad cold. Then she turned to Kathy. "Well? Did you get your folks?"

"They'll be here any minute," Kathy explained. "I told them that keeping Carly's mother's operation a secret was really crummy. They thought so, too, but they said her mom insisted."

"She thinks I'm such a baby!" Carly stamped her foot. "I could be at the hospital right now helping her—like I helped Amber."

"I know. You did a great job." Kathy faltered, then took Carly's hand. "I'm really sorry for giving you such a hard time all week. I had no idea what was on your mind."

"Me, either," Linda apologized. "I know if it had been Doña—well, I would've been worried sick. That doesn't leave much time for being a good friend."

"The worst part was I thought both of you were keeping it a secret from me, too," Carly said. "I thought I was the only one who didn't know how my own mother was."

"Well, I think you'll find out in a minute. My parents were calling the hospital before they came over. Let's hope they have good news."

"I think I hear your parents' car now," Linda said.

"Good." Kathy took Carly's hand. "Come on, let's find out what's going on."

Linda slipped Amber's halter off. The palomino shook her head and pawed the straw.

Linda laughed. "I bet you're glad there're no more shots—at least this morning," she added solemnly. "You'll just have to remember that they'll make you better."

Amber nodded as if she understood. Linda closed the stall door. She was dying to find out what was happening between Carly and the Hamiltons, but she knew it was family business, so she kept herself busy picking up the sleeping bags and giving them a good shaking.

A squeal of delighted laughter made her whirl around. Carly and Kathy were dancing and skipping down the aisle.

"Did you guys win a million dollars?" Linda joked.

"Better than that!" Carly cried. "My mom had her operation last night, and she's doing great."

She ran and jumped into Linda's arms. Kathy joined them, almost knocking Linda down.

Not wanting to be left out, Amber stuck her head over the stall partition and into the middle of the trio. Her whiskers tickled Linda's cheek, and she laughed. Carly and Kathy started laughing, too.

"Hey!" Kathy pulled away. "Isn't it great what Dr. Burnside said about Amber?"

Linda nodded happily.

"Equine influenza," Carly replied, pronouncing the words perfectly. "She'll be as good as new—if Mac gives her her medicine."

"And if you help take care of her," Linda added.

"Oh, could I?" Carly's eyes glowed. It was the first time Linda had ever seen her enthusiastic about something she or Kathy had suggested.

"Amber insists," Linda said. She stroked Amber's cheek, and the mare gave Carly a nudge with her nose. Carly stumbled, but instead of shrieking with anger she turned and gave Amber a hug.

"Boy, for someone who was scared to death of horses, you sure changed fast," Linda said.

"Well, Amber's pretty special." Carly patted the mare's golden neck.

Linda nodded. "Yep, she's pretty special," she agreed. She ruffled Amber's silky mane. In a soft voice that only Amber could hear, she added, "But then, I always knew that, didn't I?"